Addicted to You

Stories Of Spice

Melissa Current

Published by Melissa Current, 2024.

STORIES OF SPICE

First edition. March 6, 2024.

ISBN: 979-8224321186

Written by Melissa Current.

Table of Contents

Thank you to all my family and friends who have supported me in my journey! Thank you to all the amazing people who read my books!

Chapter 1 Harper

*S**mack*, his warm hand lands hard on my ass cheek and a wave of pleasure runs through my body. A loud moan escapes my lips followed by a breathy "Again". *Smack, smack,* His hand smacks down again and again, God it feels so fucking good. His hand rubs the heated skin on my ass then travels lower to settle between my legs on my bare cunt. I grasp the legs of the table I am bent over in anticipation of what's coming. Moans fall from my lips as his finger rubs on my aching clit. Cries of pleasure come as he slides his fingers into my hot folds and rubs my g spot. My wrists rub against the padded shackles while I struggle to hold still as pleasure races through my body.

A small whimper escapes my lips as his touch leaves me. He returns by taking a long slow lick and then sucking my clit into his mouth. He sucks vigorously, I feel myself close to release. *Smack,* His hand comes down again as his tongue attacks my clit, I scream out in pleasure as my orgasm rips through me and my body feels limp.

"I'm going to fuck you like the good little whore you are" he says, his husky voice full of lust and want.

"Please" I beg. I want him to fuck me; it has been far too long since I have had him.

I hear his belt and then his zipper, I groan with desire as I lay there shackled to the table waiting. I have waited for months to have this again, I am so tired of waiting, I am so desperate for another release. *Smack,* his hand lands hard down on my pussy, it makes me gasp but I follow it with a loud "more".

"Hold still for me baby cakes" he groans in my ear before thrusting his hard dick inside my pussy all the way to the hilt. He bucks his hips faster and harder as he wraps his hand in my long brunette hair and pulls my head back to give him better leverage.

"Yes. Fuck me" I moan "More" I cry out

"Be a good little whore for me" he says as he smacks my ass again

My pussy starts to spasm, I grasp the table legs, my arousal drips from me as my orgasm rocks through my body. He continues thrusting until he rides out his release and fills me, I lay there breathless.

"SO, ARE YOU STILL WITH him" Jax asks me with a raised brow and buttoning up his dark blue jeans.

"Yes" I tell him as I pull my navy-blue V-neck back on so I can fix my hair.

"Why do you stay with him Harper?" He asks trying to hide his annoyance.

"He's good to me Jax and he wants a relationship." I answer pulling out my curling iron to reset my long curls.

"Yet you call me when you want a good fuck" He whispers in my ear and gives my ass a squeeze as he walks by me on his way to my tiny kitchen to grab a beer.

His hot breath on my ear sends a spark of heat through my body and desire hits at my core again. I wouldn't have to seek him out for great sex if he wasn't so stubborn. I don't know why he has a hang up with relationships. Jax Adams had a stubborn streak a mile wide and the front of your typical bad boy. His tall and lean hard body connects to a set of broad shoulders and massive biceps. His hard frame is covered in tattoos adding to that sexy bad boy image complete with a bit of a rap sheet. His dark brown eyes turn almost black when they fill with desire. He drips with dominance and sex appeal making him just about the perfect specimen. I knew the real him though, he would dominate me in the bedroom, but he was gentle, and his heart was pure. Our sex was amazing, according to him he didn't want anyone else, he just refused to get any more serious than that and I wanted the title.

"That's because you satisfy me Jax, but Tony wants a girlfriend" I say matter of factly as if what I'm doing isn't fucked up in the least.

"Hey, I told you I didn't want to fuck anyone else but you baby cakes, but you got hung up on a stupid title." He says with his irritation front and center

"I want a boyfriend Jax, and I wanted you to spend more time not doing things that could get you thrown in jail. You know the deal." I confess, it wasn't all about the relationship, mostly though, but it was about him being reliable and stable, not in a jail cell. I know it was all petty crime stuff like paraphernalia and shoplifting, so when he did get busted, he never did much time, but the possibility of it all the time really sucked.

"Well, want in on hand baby cakes" he says as he walks over to me and places a firm hold on my throat. He leans in and takes my earlobe in between his teeth then gives it a soft suck before whispering, "Be a good whore and get on the bed," and I am all too eager to obey his command.

Chapter 2 Harper

I grab a lavender bath bomb from underneath my sink and toss it in the extra hot bath water I prepared. I am in desperate need of soothing my aching muscles, not to mention the tender skin on my ass. After the first round with Jax I was already sore, but the second one left me laying on the bed unable to move for an hour. I climb into the tub and sink down into the hot water; I let out a loud sigh as I feel the soothing water wrap around my skin. Holy fuck that was great, but I am going to feel it for a few days.

After taking my long soak in my tub, I pull on a black silk night dress, I can't handle anything to restrictive right now. I continue on with my Friday night routine which consists of popcorn, beer, and true crime documentaries. As I settle into my bed I smile and feel a hint of arousal start to creep in as I get a whiff of his musky smell that is lingering on my sheets. Fuck he always smells so damn good. I'm going to have to wash my sheets before Tony comes over again. I finally settle on a documentary and start shoving my face full of popcorn trying to fight of the desire to call Jax again. I know my poor body couldn't handle it, but arousal consumes me just the same.

"HARPER LYNN KENNEDY" I hear from the other end of the phone as soon as I answer it

"Hey Kellie" I say calmly. Fuck, the cats out of the bag now. I should have known that Jax wouldn't keep his mouth shut when it came to his sister. She wanted us to be together just as much as I did, sometimes more it seemed. Kellie was force of nature and always was a little outspoken. We've known each other since we were kids, and we were still close. I just still wanted to keep my cheating hook ups with her sexy ass brother a secret. Jax clearly didn't feel the same.

"Oh, don't you, hey Kellie me you sexy little slut. When the hell were you going to tell me, you were fucking my brother again?" she says playfully

"It's only every few months. Sometimes I just need him. It was staying a secret, but I guess he couldn't resist." I confess to her

"I still don't know why both of you can't get your heads out of your asses and figure out that you belong together." she says

"He just can't commit Kellie" I say trying not to sound too sad about it.

"Honey, only fucking you, and no one else is committed for an Adams man. That's like... a huge deal." Kellie reminds me. She has made that statement plenty of times and unfortunately it was true.

"You talk like it's a requirement for your family Kellie" I chuckle

"Well, what do you expect. They're like all criminals Harper not husbands, they run the risk of going to jail every day, they also love sex, it's just who they are." She says with her, it is what it is, attitude.

"You say that like you guys are a fucking no commitment, criminal sex club or some shit" I say with laughter.

"That's fucking hilarious, my dad would love that" she laughs "hey I'll come see you next weekend ok"

"k, bye" I say as I hang up. "Fucking Jax!" I say out loud as I rummage my medicine cabinet for some aspirin. Why the fuck did he blab to Kellie?

We have had this arrangement for a while now and I wanted it to stay a secret. The less people who know the better. A few years ago, when I gave up on the hope that Jax and I would be anything more two people who have fucking amazing sex together, I stopped going around. I kept in contact with Kellie, but I tried to keep some distance. That's when I met Tony. He was nice, clean cut, and I didn't have to worry about him ending up in jail. He wants a future with me, and he has the job to provide.

Jax always provided, I mean I never went without. I have my house because of him and my car. The house is small but it's mine, I own it. Until I met Jax I had never owned anything in my life. I guess everything I have is because of him in a way. He just never seemed to come by money in the legal way. With Tony everything is on the up and up. Well, everything except the sex.

Tony is stable, and predictable. He wants to be in a relationship with me, and it would be security if we were to ever have kids. I never had any of those things growing up. My family was fucked up. My dad was a junkie and absent most of the time and my mom wasn't much better. She drank all the time, had a new boyfriend every month or so, and we were always moving because she always ended up drinking away the rent. Jax and Kellie eventually convinced their family to take me in. They saved me, but that is still not the life I would want for any child. I need the stability and less dysfunction, even if it comes with unfulfilling sex.

Chapter 3 Jax

"You fucking did what!" Kellie yells at me "I can't believe you Jax, What the fuck were you thinking"

"Don't be like that Kellie, you know I only want her" I say trying to justify my actions. I mean she calls me, but I always go running.

"Then all you had to do was be her boyfriend Jax." She snaps.

"Fuck Kellie, don't start with that! Why did we need a fucking label on it? Why do girls always have to fuck shit up with titles?" I say knowing that it really would have been that simple and I was diffidently way too stubborn, but so was Harper.

"Look, Jax, I understand in our family it's normal, I mean fuck, Mom and Dad still aren't married, but Harper has wanted "normal" since we were kids. So, she may be stubborn and ridiculous about it at times but that's her dream and she wanted that with you. She loves you, but she wanted commitment. She has that now." Kellie is stern in her words, but that shit eating grin she has on her face tells me she excited about it and no doubt heading outside to call Harper right now. I fucking hate it when she's right though, I probably should leave well enough alone but Harper's like a fucking addiction.

I probably shouldn't have told Kellie because I'm going to hear about it from Harper, but I had to tell somebody. Kellie and Harper were pretty close, so I was hoping to maybe see if there was any way to maybe win her back. I really can't resist her. She calls and I run to her, every time no matter what I'm doing. I know she's with Tony and he's safe and shit, but he can't satisfy her. My baby needs handled right, and I know how to do that, not fucking Tony. I don't know why she wastes her time with that guy anyway. That's a fucking lie, I know why, she's with him because I couldn't commit to anything more than fucking only her. I don't want to be with anyone else, and I haven't been. Not even in the in the first two years after Harper left. How's that for fucking commitment.

The first time she called my heart about beat right out of my chest. I was so nervous I almost stumbled over my words making an ass of myself. When she told me she needed to see me I was there, no questions asked. When I saw the tears in her eyes when she opened the door, I was ready for blood. I laughed out loud when she told me the tears were just form the lack of sexual pleasure for two years. When I gave her a hug for comfort and she leaned in and whispered "I'll be a good little whore for you" my dick got so hard I couldn't resist the urge to rip her skimpy, silk night gown right down the middle and hoist her up on my hips and suck her hardened nipple right into my mouth as I carried her to the bed.

It had been so long since I had her, I took my time. Kissing and biting every inch of her breasts, and then all the way down to her hot soaking wet pussy. I sucked her clit right into my mouth and I savored that shit. She wrapped her fingers up in my hair pulling me in closer to her sweet cunt. Uncontrollable moans fell from her lips as I traveled lower and licked around her ass, when I slid my fingers inside her dripping pussy I kept my thumb on her clit. Every bit of her was being ravished, I pumped my fingers vigorously as I sucked and licked her ass. Her pussy started to spasm around my fingers, and her release was soon dripping from her. I took my pants off as fast as I could, she was so ready for me to fuck her.

"Roll over" I commanded her, and my good girl obeyed.

I grabbed her hips and positioned her ass in the air. I lined my dick up in the center of her hot folds, I slid my finger up her pussy getting it wet, then I started rubbing soothing circles between her ass cheeks. With one hard thrust of my hips, I slammed my hard cock deep inside of her as I continue massaging her. I inched my finger inside and a pleasure filled "Yes" escaped her. I continued thrusting and fingering, her screams got louder and louder. I could feel my release coming soon.

"Harder, I'll be your good little whore" She moaned out and with her words I found my release. I rode out my orgasm and collapsed next to her on the bed. I pulled her in close to me and we drifted off to sleep.

It was from that point on we had an arraignment. When she really needed it and Tony was going to be away for a while Harper could call. I know it's wrong and fucked up, but I need her just as much as she needs me. I need to find a way to get her back, without a fucking title.

Chapter 4 Harper

I wake to the sound of my alarm ringing in my head. The bed groans as I sit up to find my slippers. I let out a yawn and I wince a little through it as the stretch that comes with it pulls my still incredibly sore muscles. I guess I'll be having aspirin with breakfast again. Today is welcomed, it's Monday so I can get back to work and have a good distraction from Jax. I have to get back to reality before Tony gets back to town. Today will be busy, it's the first day of October so that means we get to change everything over to our fall menu at the coffee shop I manage.

I love this time of year, the cool crisp air in the mornings, apple crisp and pumpkin spice everything, and the beautiful yellows and reds of the changing leaves. Everyone starts decorating with scarecrows, pumpkins and straw bales getting ready to kick off all the holiday craft fairs. My favorite part is the warm clothes. I get to get out all of my favorite hooded sweatshirts, flannels, cute hats and bear paw boots. Fall is probably my favorite season.

When I get to work, I am greeted with a smiling face and a hot pumpkin spice breve.

"Well, tell me what you think boss" Amy says cheerfully. I think she loves Fall just as much as I do

"Amy that's perfect, thank you so much!" I tell her after tasting her masterpiece.

"I couldn't wait! I just had to open the boxes and give the new stuff a try" She cheers "also, all the boxes are in the storeroom ready to be entered into the inventory and I pulled all the old menus. Oh, and I decorated the menu board for fall."

"Thank you. Let's get to work then" I cheer with excitement.

I HAD SPENT THE DAY decorating, changing over inventory, and deciding what the specials will be for the month I didn't even realize it was closing time. The shop looks pretty great, not to brag on myself or anything. It was such a welcomed distraction, but the Aspirin I took at lunch was starting to wear off and I could use a good hot bath. After a quick stop at the store for some necessities, also known as dinner from the deli, I make my way home.

After my not-so-great ready-made dinner I get my bath prepared. I go for a rose bubble bath paired with a glass of cheap wine and a movie on my phone. The warm water from the bath wraps around me, hugging every inch of my skin and a soothing sensation flows through my body. The rose bubbles offered up a relaxing aroma, breathing it in deep brought me peace. My little escape to paradise was soon interrupted by the sound of my text messages. I let out a groan of disappointment as I pick up my phone to see who it was. I want to ignore it, but I haven't heard from Tony his whole trip so far and I really don't want to miss his check in. My heart flutters in my chest a little when I see it's Jax.

Dammit he shouldn't get to me like that. My feelings betray me; there is no future with Jax. He doesn't want commitment. I want a husband and kids someday. Jax can't offer me that, especially not honestly. Jax and the other Adams men are known in the area for their shady lifestyle. Their shady pawn shops provide store fronts to sell all the merchandise they usually get by the "fell off the back of a truck" method. There are also their drug dealings, as if being thieves wasn't bad enough. I'm also pretty confident that the first car he got me was from his uncle's chop shop, maybe even the one I have now.

My shelter has been on behalf of his family in one way or another from the time I was 16. I had lousy parents and an unstable home life, I'm not even sure my mom ever noticed I was gone, I mean I don't recall her ever coming to look for me. They took me in, offered me a room and food, Kellie even stole me my clothes until I learned enough to do it myself. Jax's mom gave me my first cigarette, and his dad offered me my first beer. It was dysfunctional, but stable. There was love and kind words, it may have been praise for the good job you did stealing a TV or selling a bag of drugs, but it was kind just the same and made me feel wanted. I just can't understand why Jax could provide me with everything I wanted, a house, a car, furnishings, and even only having sex with me, but he couldn't commit to calling it a relationship.

Looking at the message he wrote sends my stomach into knots but a blush to my cheeks. I feel my body temperature rise enough that I am sure it could reheat my bath water. The message simply read:

Hey baby cakes. I have grown tired of our arrangement. I want you back and I will get what I want. I will get to shackle you to that table anytime I want.

I don't even know how to process that information.

Chapter 5 Jax

"Jax, did you and Hector get that car in last night?" Ricky asked as he opened the door, his voice echoed through the garage and pulled me from the tire I was changing.

"Ya, it's in the back" I yell back at him. My older brother Ricky helps my cousin Kenny run a tire shop, the heat was on my uncle Mick a few years back, so he had to shuffle things around. The tire shop runs a much more honest business. There is a warehouse out back where we keep the tire inventory, but it also serves as the intake for the other garages. I work here to part time so I can show an honest paycheck, and I run cars on the weekends for Kenny and Ricky. I started running cars after Harper left, I needed more of a thrill since I was majorly lacking sexual satisfaction. She poured her heart and soul into the coffee shop, became the manager and tried to convince herself that she didn't need me, while I took my crimes to the next level. My dad wants me to take over one of the pawn shops, but I don't know if I want that yet, or at all.

"Ok. Have it ready to move tonight!" He bellowed. If it wasn't for the fact that he's my brother and he has always come off as a loud fucking ass, I might have thought he was mad. He was 6' 3" and he was fucking built, that fucker lived at the gym. Those stupid muscle shirts he wore helped draw plenty of attention to him. The girls practically spread their legs on the spot for him, and he was always more than happy to accept the offers.

"Ya, ya, ya. I will." I mutter under my breath getting back to work.

"JAX, ARE YOU FUCKING sure about this?" Hector questions me as we start making preparations to move the car.

"Fuck ya!" I answer confidently

"Ok. It's just she's a good girl, she's not like us man. She's got a real job and everything" he says lightheartedly but there's an underlying seriousness in his voice.

"I've got to get her back Hector. She's all I want." I say knowing that he's going to give me his honest opinion and I may not like it. That is why I talk to him though. Hector and I go way back to grade school, we grew up together, hell we even went to jail together. He's honest and lets me know what's up. He was there for me when Harper left, let me sleep on his couch for a while even.

"I'm just saying she deserves to be happy and have a good life is all" he says, and I know his concern for her Is genuine.

"She also deserves to be pleasured the way she wants; she shouldn't have to hide that side of her!" I say and the words come out a little more frustrated than I would like.

"How the fuck do you know she's not?" he questions with a sharp tone and his brows furrowed

"Because I'm the one who's been doing it." I confess bracing for the earful I am about to get.

"You're Fucking sleeping with her again! What the fuck are you thinking Jax?" He starts scolding me and it makes me feel like a child. "Why the fuck would you do that. She has a boyfriend who wants a future with her. That's all Harper has ever wanted Jax it can't just be about sex." He continues, his tone is firm, and his face is scowled in disappointment. It makes me angry, but I listen.

"She fucking called me, first off, and I do want a future with her dammit!" I yell, emotions flaring "I bought her a fucking house, I lived with her, I got her a reliable car so she could get downtown because she wanted a real job. I wanted her and only her, I just didn't want to put a fucking label on it. Why the fuck is that so wrong?" I say unloading on Hector as if he's the reason for losing Harper. It's my fault, I know it is, but I don't like it when it gets pointed out she moved on to Tony, if that's even what you want to call it.

"The label means the world to her Jax. To her that means commitment and stability. I told you she's not like us. She had a shit life, and we got her into some shit situations, but she is good and wants a good life." He pauses for a moment before continuing on with probably the most valid question of the night.

"What the fuck can you really offer if you don't want to call it what it is and clean up your life a little. Does she even know you're here, helping the chop shop? Honest answer Jax." He asks, his tone softer but his expression lets me know he can see through any bullshit I try to feed him right now. I know he's right but that doesn't make it hurt less.

I offer him a simple "no" because it's the truth. Harper doesn't know I'm here; she would fucking kill me. She wanted me to stay out of jail and this, this is actual time in prison, not a few weeks here or there in county. I know I should listen to him, he's right. I don't bring much stability to the table and asking her to consider raising kids while I'm in and out of jail isn't fucking very fair, but I fucking love her, I have since we were young. I have to let her know that that's better than any fucking label, that's fucking real shit.

"We better get back to work" Hector says offering me a smile and handing me the tool bag.

Chapter6 Harper

"Who the fuck does he think he is" I say to myself as I shuffle through the end of the night receipts and paperwork that cover my desk. What the fuck is Jax thinking. He interrupted my bath, and then my sleep two nights in a row, now I can't even concentrate on my work. I don't even know what to think about it all, he can't commit so why would he want me back. Tony is due to be home tonight and Jax is supposed to leave me alone after a good fuck. He is supposed to stay out of sight until I get a wild horny hair and call him again, not tell his fucking sister about it and make it public knowledge. He was sure as hell not supposed to decide to change our agreement. My stomach stirs and the knots grow stronger, there was so much unpredictability now, what if he shows up, what if he tells Tony? I grab some club soda and some flavoring in hopes that an Italian soda will help calm my stomach. I grab my jacket and lock up for the night deciding that the paperwork can wait until morning.

The soda and the drive home seem to help calm my nerves, but I am still upset. Why does he think he can just decide now to fuck up a good thing? It's not the right thing to be doing but it's an arrangement that I can live with. I get to have a future with commitment and stability without criminal charges lingering, as well as a much-needed hard kinky fuck. Neither man can seem to offer me both, otherwise I wouldn't be in this position.

When I pull into my driveway I am surprised when I see Tony's car on the street. I didn't think he would be back in town until later tonight and he usually spends his first night home at his apartment in the city. I am greeted at the door with flowers, Roses to be exact and a bottle of expensive wine.

"Hey Hun, how was your week?" Tony asks with his award winning bright white smile, we had been together for a while before I learned he had spent the money to get veneers, he said he wanted to look his best in his photo for his business card. I guess when you sell luxury apartments in the cities you want to look your best. I admit he is a handsome man; he is clean cut with piercing blue eyes and a sharp Jaw. His blond hair was kept short, and he kept his small frame covered in suits and preppy sweaters. Handsome, yes, Jax Adams sexy, no.

"It was good, I did a lot of decorating at the shop and got everything switched over for fall, so it was productive. Thank you for the flowers." I say with a warm smile. I do love the flowers, Lilies are my favorite, but Tony thinks they aren't as romantic as roses. I have never been big on fancy expensive wine, but the gesture is sweet. He tries, and I appreciate it.

I start nervously rummaging through my kitchen to find a vase to put the roses in. Tony is here with both roses and wine; he is also still in his suit. Something is up I just know it. He never wears his Ralph Lauren, or Armani, or whichever fucking stupid designer he's wearing, I never gave a fuck about any of that shit. He won't even wear them of dates, he always tells me it's because I don't have anything to wear that would come close to matching it, at the same time reminding me he could buy something for me if I was worried about the price. I usually just try to play it off as I'm too proud to accept it instead of telling him that I am just not into that fucking shit, and the fact he thinks it's about money is slightly insulting. I want stability, I don't want to look stuck up and superficial, I am a jeans and leggings type of girl. I finally find where I stashed my vase and prepare the water for the roses when Tony places a piece of paper on the counter and tells me to look at it.

"What's this?" I ask looking at a paper with a beautiful luxury apartment listing on it. It had a huge open floor plan that was naturally lit by huge windows that showcased the stunning view of the city. The kitchen was huge and full of stainless-steel appliances to match the gray tones of the paint and the floors. The master bathroom had a gorgeous walk-in shower with a waterfall shower head, in the corner was a beautiful sunken jacuzzi tub that I could almost envision myself soaking in right now. The walk-in closet looked like it was the size of a whole bedroom, I could never fill that thing. It was a beautiful place, but didn't give a very homey feel.

"Do you like it?" Tony asks almost giddy

"Well, it's beautiful and huge" I start to explain and am quickly cut off by Tony before I can even finish my thought

"Good, because I just bought it for us!" He exclaims

"You what?" I question him almost chocking on the words

"I looked at it this week while I was in Seattle" he says so proudly

"I-I-It's in Seattle" I stumble over the words trying to process what the fuck he is saying. I don't understand, why would he buy an apartment in Seattle for us, especially without talking to me first. I have told him I love it here, I love my job, and I love living outside of the city.

"Yes, Isn't it great!" He says as he pours us each a glass of the expensive wine he brought. He hands me one and extends his up in an attempt to toast.

"Oh, ya great." I say flatly "So you are moving?" I question looking for more answers and explanation

"No silly, we are moving. I transferred so I don't have to travel so much." he says gulping down the whole glass of wine he poured seemingly in one swallow. "Isn't that awesome!" He cheers

"Uh...Ya sure...Uh, can I take some time to process this all please. I mean that's a lot, I have a job and a house, and my friends." I say starting to feel panic rise and my stomach fall and knot up again. I don't really want to fight right now though so I throw in "It is just such a big surprise honey" and give him a hug and a kiss on the cheek.

"Alright, sweetie." He says giving me a small kiss "It's going to be great. We can start fresh, hardly any packing required. I'll see you tomorrow ok." He says as he heads to the door.

"Right. Tomorrow." I say as I close the door. What the actual fuck, I feel slightly betrayed, was he even thinking of me at all. I don't want to move, I don't want to live in a fancy apartment in the city, he really should know that I've mentioned that before, we stay at my place most of the time because of it. Fuck, this day just needs to be over.

Chapter 7 Harper

"Any plans after work tonight?" Amy cheerfully asks as she pulls her pink zip up jacket on preparing to leave for the night. She was always so cheery and bright, like nothing could ever drag her down. She was about the best barista I had. I was drawn to her bubbly, easygoing personality from the second she stepped in here for the interview and I am so grateful I hired her. She lives in pink; she also makes it her mission to put a smile on everyone's face. She always gets amazing reviews from the customers and keeps staff entertained and motivated. I was so excited when the owner and I came up with new designs for out uniform tee shirts. I got to order them in more colors than just black and gray, so I made sure to add pink as well as navy blue. The look on her face was priceless when she opened up the box and realized she could choose pink. She will make an amazing manager someday, I guess maybe sooner than I was thinking.

"Not really, just my usual Friday night, bubble bath, popcorn and true crime" I chuckle. When really, I know it will be another sleepless night and avoiding an important talk with Tony. He is still waiting for me to answer him, and I really don't want to.

"You and your true crime addiction" she laughs as she heads out of the shop.

I finish getting everything ready for the crew that will be in tomorrow morning and gather my things. As I walked outside the autumn breeze brought a pink color to my cheeks, it moved through my hair as it danced through the trees, I paused for a moment to enjoy the feeling. It was so beautiful this time of year with the leaves changing colors and falling as the trees prepare to sleep. As I make my way to my car I pull out my phone, just out of curiosity, to check the weather for Seattle...fucking rain, who would have fucking guessed.

AS I SOAK IN THE HOT water letting the bubbles tickle my skin and breathing in their warm fragrance of lilacs it takes me back to the early summer when I was 18. It was warm that night, the sky was filled with gorgeous hints of pink and orange as the sun started to set. Jax's dad had sent the boys on an errand for the pawn shop, Kellie and I tagged along to provide a distraction while Jax and Hector got out with some electronics. Things went smooth at the first store, and we made a successful drop at the shop. The next store didn't go as smooth; we ended up being chased by the cops. Jax grabbed me by the arm pulling me to the car. We lost the cops, but we also lost Hector and Kellie as well. We ended up out in the middle of nowhere alone.

We needed to lay low for a while, so we had plenty of time to talk. Jax shared some stories of when him and hector were in grade school and they had me laughing so hard. It seemed the Adams boys were just born to be a bit rough and rowdy. They had the wrong side of the track's reputation, but nobody ever really fucked with them. They were never afraid to fight and usually came out on the winning side. But if they were close to you and accepted you, you got to know a whole different side of them, the softer side.

After talking and smoking some weed on the hood of the car for what seemed like hours, admiring the way the stars looked in the summer sky, Jax confessed to something that took me by surprise but set my heart and body on fire. He told me that he had been crushing on me for a while now and wanted to kiss me. I was so nervous, he was so sexy, I was so afraid that I would mess it up. That first kiss was fire; it sent an aching sensation straight to my center. It was like instant chemistry. His rough hands explored my body, but they felt soft and gentle, his touch was magic and sent sparks through me.

His kisses started to travel lower, eventually landing on my neck, it ignited my belly with a desire I had never felt before. I wanted him, I needed him, in that moment I had to have him, all of him. With his hand caressing my breast, and open mouth kisses on my neck soft moans fell from my lips that I couldn't control. My core felt hot and wet, lust filled my eyes, I locked my gaze on his dark brown eyes and all I could breathe out was "Please". A lust filled groan is all he replied with to the permission I had just granted him.

His hands moved lower and grabbed the button on my jeans, once my zipper was opened his hand slid down into my black lace panties. My breath hitched in my throat as his finger found my clit.

"More" I begged, and he was more than happy to give it.

He slid my pants down and pulled me closer to the edge of the hood. He started planting soft kisses up my legs. I was so ready for him to ravage me. He took a long slow lick, I couldn't hold in my pleasure, I had never felt this before, loud pleasure filled moans escaped me as he sucked my clit into his mouth. I didn't want it to end but when he slid his two fingers into my warm folds and pumped them while his tongue worked my clit I couldn't help but find my release.

He laid beside me and crashed his lips against mine, and I parted my lips to allow his amazing tongue to slip in. His kiss was so full of passion it made me ache for more. I ran my fingers down his chest to his belt. I undid his buckle, then the button on his jeans, I gasped a little when I felt his hardened cock for the first time. Soft moans escape him as my hand pumped up and down. I felt his hot breath at my ear, and it was electrifying, he simply whispered "can I fuck you baby cakes?"

Through heavy panting a simple "ya" is all I could whimper. I was so overtaken by lust in that moment I felt tipsy and unable to think straight I just knew I need to feel more of him. He dropped his pants and lined his hard dick up at my center, he inched in slowly, I winced in pain, but it felt so fucking good.

"You ok baby" He asked with genuine concern in his voice

"Yes, please don't stop" I said reassuring him.

He kept his movements slow and steady at first and I moaned out with pleasure. He leaned in and sucked my nipple into his mouth and a whimper fell from my lips. His pace quickened and every kiss was filled with intensity, it was raw, and it was magic. My moans were timed to his thrusts, and my breathing grew faster, I felt like I was going to explode.

"More Jax" I scream out feeling myself right on the edge of release. He placed the pad of his thumb on my hardened nub and my release came uncontrollably. My toes curled, my head fell back, and my body went numb, I held him close to me as he rode out his release.

My thighs clench tightly and the bath water almost spills over the side of my tub as I find my release to the memory of our first time, my first time. Every sexual awakening I have ever had was at the hands of Jax Adams. The first time he smacked my ass I was so embarrassed that I liked it so much.

My phone pings and pulls me from my thoughts. I stand up to pull my soft black robe over my wet shoulders and step out onto my bathmat. Sliding my feet into my matching slippers, my chest rises and falls as I take a deep breath, not sure if I am prepared to see who it was that messaged me. My heart flutters a little bit, and a blush rises to my cheeks as I read his message:

Hey Baby Cakes! I can't wait to Fuck You again. I'm thinking a surprise visit may be in order. My dick is getting hard just thinking of your naked body bound and spread for me.

Chapter 8 Jax

I send the message knowing that it would get to her. We excite each other and neither one of us can deny that. I grab a towel so I can shave and take a shower. I'm getting a little scruffy and I want to look good for my girl. She likes it when I keep my goatee trimmed up, and she gets wet for my cologne. I know what turns her on and I am going to use that to my advantage right now. I can't risk that fuck face Tony winning. Harper is mine, she has always been mine, from that very moment I took her on the hood of my old car that night. She was amazing, she tasted amazing, she was pure. I was her first and I felt fucking honored, Harper Kennedy was fucking gorgeous, she had long brown hair, and her hazel eyes would intoxicate you when you looked into them. She only stood about 5'4" but she had a slender waist and a luscious ass. She could have had so many guys, but she wasn't like that.

I wasn't even sure she was going to let me kiss her that night, but I desperately wanted to try. I thought I was a lucky guy when I got to taste her sweet lips. She kissed me with such passion and desire, I had never been kissed like that before, it was like electricity sparking through my body. The way she looked into my eyes that night and asked "please" filled my body with lust and desire, it made my dick instantly hard, and I craved her. I was addicted to her, to the chemistry we had, to the lust I saw in her eyes at that moment. I have to get her back, I must!

I SNEAK IN QUIETLY since I don't see that assholes car out front. She looks so fucking sexy sleeping in that short red silk night gown, it doesn't cover her ass all the way, so I have a perfect view of her red lace panties. Her ass looks so inviting, I pull my pants off to free my hard cock. The bed groans as I climb in next to her, I run my hands up her legs and stop at her ass. I lean in slowly and take her earlobe in my mouth to take a hard suck. I whispered in her ear "I'm going to fuck you baby cakes!"

"I was expecting you" was her only reply as she rolled to gain access to my lips. I climb on top of her and pin her arms above her head as I slowly nibble at her neck and her collar bone. I let my mouth slowly travel down to her breasts and soft moans fall from her lips as I suck on her pebbled nipple. I release her hands so I can travel lower, I need a taste of that sweet pussy of hers. Her fingers tangle in my hair and a breathless "yes" escapes her as I move her panties to the side and take a long languid lick. Fuck she tastes so good. I take her clit between my tongue and my teeth; she pulls on my hair but holds me closer wanting more.

I lick and suck at her clit as I slide my fingers inside her hot folds thrusting them hard and fast like she likes. I listen with pride as her uncontrollable moans keep coming. I want to send her over the edge so I do something I know will get to her. I move my mouth to her ass attacking it with my tongue and place my thumb on her clit, she screams out in pleasure as all of her is being ravaged. Her release comes in waves, her hands pull my hair, her toes cure and her thighs try to clench, "OH FUCK" she screams as she drips with the pleasure, I just gave her. I chuckle with delight knowing that I am the only one that can give her this.

As she catches her breath I go to the closet to get some rope, I haven't tied her hands to the bed in a while, and I know she likes it. I toss the red velvet rope on the bed next to her and command her to roll over. Her eyes fill with lust and her lips curl up into her perfect smile.

"I promise I'll be a good little whore" she says rolling over and extending her hands to the headboard. Fuck, I love it when she talks like that.

With her hands tied to the bed and her lush ass propped up for me, I am ready to tease her. *Smack*, my hand comes down on her ass cheek.

"More" she groans softly as my hand connects with her ass again.

I take a long hard lick of her sweet pussy, and it clenches a little as she braces for what she knows is coming.

"Yes" she screams as my hand smacks against her soaking center "Again" she screams "please", and I refuse to disappoint her.

It makes me so hard, and I want nothing more than to slam my dick into her right fucking now, but I fight that urge. My baby likes to beg, and this night is about her. I have to do anything I can to get Harper back, so I will be patient and wait for her. She may be bound but she is the one in control. *Smack*, my hand makes contact again and again, finally the words fall from her lips "Please Jax, fuck me."

At her request I ready my dick at her dripping folds and dig my fingers into her hips.

"How baby cakes" I ask hoping she will give the answer I am longing for.

"Hard! Please, I fucking need you" she pants. My lips curl into a smile, that was exactly the answer I wanted.

With one hard thrust I fill her walls all the way and hard moans escape us both. She feels so fucking good. My nails dig into her skin as my grip gets tighter and tighter. My pace quickens as I slam into her over and over, faster and faster. She screams out my name as her pussy spasms, I feel her release dripping all over. I fucking love it when I do that to her. I keep my pace quick and my breathing changes as I feel myself about to let go. My head falls, and my toes start to tingle as I fell myself filling her fully. We collapse on the bed, out of breath and fulfilled. I untie the rope and pull Harper's naked body against mine and without even thinking about it I whisper "I love you" before drifting off to sleep.

Chapter 9 Harper

I can't even open my mouth to respond, did he really just say that, better yet did he really mean it. Jax has never said "I love you" to me before, ever. It always comes in the form of "you are mine" or "I only want you." It makes me want him; it makes me miss what I had with him and makes me feel very conflicted. I know I have to answer Tony, and a part of me thinks I should move with him. It is safe, reliable, and the apartment really is beautiful. There is another part of me that thinks I love it here, maybe Jax really will commit to me, maybe it just took him a while to grow up, and also maybe I was too hard on him. He said he loves me, maybe the stupid title really doesn't matter, he loves me, that's probably enough, no that is enough. I sink down into his arms and join him in sleep.

I AM AWAKENED BY THE sound of Jax's phone, I am sleepy, but I overhear part of the conversation.

"Hey Jax, I know its late, but Kenny may have a run for you tomorrow, can you give Hector a heads up?" I recognize the voice on the other end of the line. It's Ricky, but what does he mean by run?

"Ya, no problem, man. I'll catch up with you tomorrow" Jax says hanging up the phone.

"What was that about?" I ask Jax with furrowed brows

"Well, I may need to fill in and help Ricky" Jax says nervously like he wants to hide something

"Fill in how Jax" I push

"Baby, um" Jax starts to explain, and I already know where this is heading. What the hell is he thinking? That's fucking prison time!

"Are you fucking kidding me Jax!" I yell. I could fucking kill him right now. He tells me he loves me just for me to find out he wants to go run cars what the fuck!

"Baby, please don't be like that. I don't have to do it anymore; Hector can handle it" he says trying reach for me.

"Anymore, what the fuck does that mean?" I scowl. How fucking long has he kept this from me? Why did he keep this from me? A feeling of betrayal washes over me.

"Hector and I help on the weekends some. It gave me a rush. I primarily work honestly now though I swear." he says trying to smooth things over

"A rush! What kind of fucking rush are you going to get in fucking prison Jax! You could get years for that!" I say with a belly full of anger and a chest full of hurt. I can't believe he is risking being apart for that long. My heart breaks at the thought of losing him like that and I am so angry that he would play such a risky game.

"I'm always careful baby cakes. I don't have to do it anymore. Kenny said they have a full-time position at the tire shop and its mine if I want it, it would be all honest work for us." He says and I know he Is just trying to reassure me, but I am so overwhelmed with emotion it's like I can't control it.

"How could you fucking do this to me Jax? You told me you loved me for the first time ever, you insist that you want to win me back, but you are fucking do this. You are playing with my emotions right now! You are a fucking ass hole!" I scream at him unable to stop any word vomit that might decide to escape my lips.

"I'm sorry, do fucking what to you exactly Harper? I fucking love you! You fucking left me! You moved someone else right on into your bed! I didn't do that shit. I haven't fucked anyone else since that fucking night with you on the hood of my car! You chose to not have a fucking say so in my fucking life anymore! If anyone is playing with anyone's emotions Harper Kennedy its fucking, you!" He says harshly and it fucking hurt. Deep down I knew it was true, but I am too stubborn to admit any wrongdoing right now.

"You have to have emotions to play with in the first fucking place Jax! If you really loved me, you would have committed to me, you would have called it what it was! The only person you care about is yourself!" I say harshly, I see his face fall like I crushed him, and I instantly regret it. That was fucked up and I know it.

"Fuck you Harper! I have always loved you, I didn't want a label, but you did, fine I get it, but I never meant that I didn't want to spend every day of my life with you. I'm done running to you at your whim and not getting to have you, it hurts to fucking bad." He says as his voice breaks and with one swift slam of my door he was gone.

My tears are relentless, falling with the intensity of a summer rainstorm. What the fuck did I just do. I think I just lost Jax for good and I have nobody to blame but myself. I never should have said those things to him. It doesn't change the fact that he should have told me, or that he never should have been helping the stupid shop. What the fuck was he thinking. Anger rises again and I can't take this anymore.

I pull my red silk robe on over my shoulders and tie it; I grab my phone and head to my kitchen. After pouring myself a glass of the expensive wine Tony left the other day, I take a look around my tiny house, I love it so much, but everything is Jax here. Maybe a fresh start wouldn't be bad. Maybe I need to move on fully. If I have lost him for good, then maybe I just need to let go of all the reminders I have of him. Like Tony said a fresh start, I assume his no packing required comment was a nice way of saying my stuff was shit, but it would be a smooth transition that way. Polishing off a second glass of wine and fulled by pain and anger I pick up my phone and open my messages. I scroll to Tony and decide to give him and answer

Hi Hun, Sorry it's so late. It was just such a shock I needed time to process it. I think Seattle will be nice. We can talk about it over lunch on Monday. You can come by the shop if you would like.

Chapter 10 Jax

I am fucking crushed. How the fuck could she say that I don't have feelings. I fucking live for her. She calls and I fucking run every fucking time. She wanted a house I fucking bought her one. I saved for a long time for that shit. Ever since I met Harper I was drawn to her. She was beautiful and she was kind. She worked hard in school; I think it brought a welcomed distraction from her fucked up home life. She never let her struggles show to most. Kellie and I knew what was going on though. Finally, when she was 16 we had the opportunity to help her. Her fucking mom never even came to look for her, never reported her missing, I don't even know if she even cared enough to notice Harper wasn't there anymore.

I wanted the best for her always. She was able to get out of the life. She told me she wanted a normal job so I made sure she could do that. I made sure Uncle Mick knew what I needed, and he came through. Harper was so happy the day she came home and told me she got the job at the coffee shop; it made me so proud. I was fucking hurt when she left, we were both so stubborn. She never could get over the fact I wouldn't call her my girlfriend, and I wasn't willing to cave. I fucked it up then and I fucked it up again.

"I'LL TAKE CARE OF THE car tonight man, don't worry about it" Hector reassures me with a little too much sympathy wearing on his face

"Thanks" I say a little more flatly than I wanted to

"You going to take that full time job Kenny has open?" he asks softly almost as if he's hoping I will.

"I don't know man, if I don't have Harper to think about, I might just take over a store for my dad. I don't know" I confess. I really don't know what I want to do. I had a plan to go on the up and up for her now, I don't know.

"I think you should, it's a good job." he states his opinion but with concern

"I don't know I'll think on it for a while now. Thanks for taking care of the car." I tell him as I head to the door to leave

"Hey Jax," He stops me before I can head out

"Ya" I say turning to face him

"Are you really done running to her?" he asks with his brow cocked

"Ya. It just hurts too fucking bad to keep doing it" I say and my heart clenches in my chest at the thought of never seeing her again

"Are you in love with her?" he asks

"Yes, I am." I tell him turning back to the door

"Then fight for her, go clean and prove to her you want to be there for her. Don't Just fucking give up like that man" he says, I nod my head to him as I close the door behind me.

Maybe Hector is right, maybe I should clean up my life a little. The money from the cars was crazy good though. Maybe I could take over the pawn shop my dad wants me to but run it straight. I don't know how much it really matters at this point. I pissed Harper off, and I don't think she will ever take me back. I told her she had no say so in my life anymore and made it sound like I thought she was a slut or something. She got with Tony, but it wasn't right away, and she hasn't been with anyone else other than me. She wasn't the kind of girl to sleep around, she formed very specific kinky likes, but she wasn't a slut, I never should have made it sound that way. She has every right to be pissed at me.

On the other hand, she was the one that left though, and then when she wasn't satisfied, she called me but only for the sex. I am so fucking hurt, but I let her do it. I knew what she needed so I let her use me for it. It was great for a while, but jealousy is a fickle mistress. I needed her more and more. I guess I used her in ways too, maybe things would have played out differently if I had turned her down. If I would have offered only comfort that night instead of letting us give into our sexual desires maybe I wouldn't be in this mess, but I am so fucking addicted.

I am addicted to her passion, not just in the bedroom, but the passion she puts into everything she does. I am addicted to her big gorgeous hazel eyes and the way they darken and fill with lust when she wants me to fuck her, but also the way they sparkle and light up her whole face when she is happy. I can't get enough of those beautiful sexy lips that curl into a perfect smile, and the way they look wrapped around my dick when she sucks me dry. Harper Kennedy is my drug, my addiction, her beauty and innocence pulls me in and the pleasureful high keeps me hungry for more. I don't think I will ever be able to walk away, no matter how much it fucking hurts to stay.

Chapter 11 Harper

I woke up Monday morning feeling a little apprehensive about the decision I had made over the weekend. I know it's not the right one especially because it was made in anger and hurt. I am still so mad at Jax for his actions, but his words, they fucking crushed me. I pull my fuzzy black robe over my shoulders and tie it; I slip on the matching slippers and head to the kitchen. I need coffee now instead of waiting until I get to work. I prepare my French press and start the kettle, my eyes drift to the view from my kitchen window. The apple tree that Jax planted for me my first year here has grown a lot, it even has put on apples a few years now. My lilly garden is slightly overgrown and neglected. I have been so busy it's been hard to keep up, but it is beautiful in the summertime.

The whistle of the kettle pulled me back to the task at hand, my coffee. I pour the boiling water into the French press and let it steep while I take care of the hot mess of a head I have going on right now. I decide I'm not feeling like putting in much effort today, so I keep things to a minimum. I run a brush through my long brown hair, pull it into a messy bun and wash my face. I throw on a little mascara and some clear lip gloss. I rummage through my closet to find something warm and cozy. I settle on a dark gray hoodie with the company logo on the back and a pair of dark blue jeans, I toss them on the bed for later.

I grab a coffee cup out of the cupboard and press down the lid to the French press. A little pumpkin cheesecake syrup mixed with some half and half; it was heaven in a cup. The steam warmed my cheeks as I took my first sip, the aroma woke my senses and as I drank it, it warmed my soul. Coffee really is my favorite part of the morning, and for the last several years this tiny kitchen is where I have enjoyed it. The thought of leaving it makes me feel empty.

I TURN THE MUSIC UP loud on my morning commute trying to avoid the voice in my head that is screaming at me. The screaming realization that I just made what is probably the worst decision of my life, and I have made some really bad decisions in the past. I have chosen to try to erase an entire chapter from my life for a man I care about but truly do not love. I don't want to think about it right now so avoidance will be my tactic today, until Tony shows up for lunch anyway.

As I struggle to find a parking spot at the coffee shop, I get a little excited, I guess my half price muffin Monday idea worked. I greet Amy as I walk in and visit with a few of the regulars before I head to the office to put my things down.

"Need any help Amy" I ask as I set my things in the office

"Ya actually, Crystal just threw in another batch of Pumpkin muffins, but I think we will need some apple and blueberry too. I needed Greg to help with drinks." She cheers, completely unaffected by the rush

"No problem, consider me on muffin duty." I say with a smile

I was so busy with the muffins I didn't have any time to think or pay attention to the time so I was surprised when Greg came to tell me I had a visitor. Knots turned in my stomach as I walked to the lobby, I felt a hint of relief when I saw that it was just Kellie.

"Hey Kellie, you want a coffee?" I ask seizing the opportunity for a coffee break

"Sure, you know I'll never turn that down" she laughs

"Ok, grab that corner booth and I'll meet you there" I say pointing to one of few tables left available. I get Amy started on making us one of her signature creations and hang up my apron. After grabbing two muffins and our coffee I head to the table to sit with Kellie.

"Sorry I didn't make it over this weekend; I had a date." she says boastfully

"It's ok…wait, what…with who?" I ask with excitement and curiosity

"Hector" she whispers with glee.

"Are you fucking serious" I was so excited for her, I always thought they would be good together but neither of them ever went for it. "How did that happen?" I ask

"Well, my dad has been looking for other business ventures and Hector mentioned that there was a bar for sale downtown. My dad thought that Hector and I could run it if it pans out. We ended up going to look at it together, before I knew it, he was telling me how beautiful he thought I was and asking me on a date." she tells me

"That's fucking crazy! To you and Hector." I say raising my coffee

"It was just one date so far, but he did kiss me at the end, and he's been texting me…a lot" she says with a smile that lights her eyes and makes her face glow.

"I'm happy for you. The two of you make sense, at least I think so." I say offering her a warm smile. "Is he a good kisser?" I ask with a laugh

"So fucking good!" She giggles as a blush shows in her cheeks. We share a moment of laughter together, but I knew a different topic would be brought up. It was only a matter of time.

"What's up with you and Jax?" she finally asks

"We had a fight. He doesn't want to see me anymore." I say as tears threaten to prick my eyes.

"What about?" she asks, blatantly prying

"I found out he was running cars for Kenny and Ricky" I say with annoyance creeping back in.

"Oh ya, that. Harper you do realize that when it comes to you, he's like a junkie right? He's fucking addicted, when you left, he didn't jump into bed with someone else he found a different drug all together, he needed another rush." She says as if it made him justified in his actions. The statement also seemed to come as a bit of a passive aggressive jab towards me.

"It still makes me mad Kellie. He could go to prison for that. It's not just small-time stuff. I just can't believe he would risk that; we would be apart for so long." I say unable to hide my frustration

"You have to actually be together to be apart Harper. His risk was his own." she says directly and it fucking stings to hear. "Look, you are my best friend and always will be, but I've just got to say it. You and Jax both need to stop being so fucking stubborn. You love each other you need to fucking figure it out." The words hurt and I hate that she said them.

"Look, he said he's done with me. So, I have decided to move to Seattle with Tony. It will probably be better this way." I tell her trying to act confident in my decision.

"Are you fucking serious Harper. Seattle? What the fuck are you going to do in Seattle?" She asks obviously annoyed and shocked by the news, she also had a point, I had no fucking clue what I was going to do there.

"It's just the best option. It will be stable and predictable. I need that." I tell her sounding more like I am trying to convince myself instead of her

"So, you're just going to give up, leave just like that. Give up on love all because why... your parents fucking sucked. What fucking good is stability if there isn't love with it?" she says with disappointment

"I have to go Kellie, you just don't understand. Jax and I are done." I say desperately trying to fight back tears.

"He's fucking in love with you Harper, he will never be done with you! You fucking know it too but choose to ignore it, as if the title is what makes it real." she says bluntly as she gathers her things to leave "Thanks for the coffee" she adds as she leaves.

I was hoping the conversation would have gone better but it went about like I expected. Kellie pointed out my flaws and stubbornness, but she was right, my parents were fucked up and I created a fantasy of what I wanted in life, but it looks like I may have left out a key element in that. How good was my life really going to be if I didn't love who I was with?

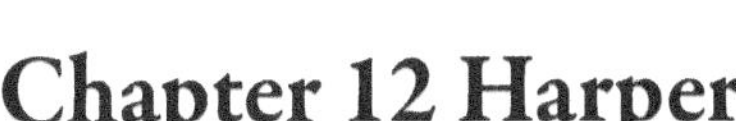

Chapter 12 Harper

A relaxing sigh leaves me as I sink down into the hot bath water. It has been an emotional week full of tension, and I am feeling it. I haven't heard form Jax at all, not that I really expected to, but I guess I was hoping. I feel empty without him around, I miss his touch, his smell, he wasn't the only one who was addicted. He was every bit my drug as I was his and I have no clue how I will go on without him. I get more and more sick to my stomach every day that goes by. I know I have made the wrong choice and now I don't know how to fix it. The two people I care about the most aren't speaking to me, and Tony is so wrapped up in moving that he hasn't even noticed that I have hardly spoken to him, or that he's stood me up for 3 lunch dates now.

My phone pings interrupting my attempt at some relaxation, I debate not even looking at it, but curiosity gets the better of me. I feel a little disappointed when I see its just Tony.

Is the door open?

yes

I hear Tony walk in and start making himself at home, I'm not sure what he's doing out there exactly but it is not helping me relax. I get out of the bath and wrap my body up in a towel. I dry off and throw on some comfy pj's so I can see what he is up to.

"What are you doing?" I ask trying to hide my annoyance at the intrusion

"I'm taking pictures and measurements; you should probably clean up your dinner dishes." Tony says as he tries to rearrange things

"Why are you doing that?" I ask as my annoyance starts to turn to complete irritation.

"Well, I'm listing the house, and the movers will be here in a week to move my furniture." He says like I should already know, but he hasn't fucking been including me in any of the planning

"A fucking week…Tony, I thought we were going to talk about this, and why are you listing my house?" I blurt out not even trying to hide emotion

"We did talk. I told you I bought an apartment in Seattle, you messaged and said Seattle sounds nice. I told you we are starting over, so we will take my furniture, and you can pack a suitcase. Oh, and I found a buyer for your car." He said it like it was no big deal

"I assumed I had more time. I haven't even talked to the coffee shop yet; I was also never told I couldn't take my car. I wasn't planning on selling my house either. Dammit Tony did you even think of me at all in any of this?" I say as I feel myself starting to spiral.

"Let's be real Harper, your car is crap and most likely came from that shady ass garage anyway, I'll get you a better one." His statement angers me, shady garage or not it was mine, who the fuck does he think he is.

"It's still mine Tony. I own it, why wouldn't you ask me, and why are you trying to sell my fucking house?" I say my voice raised bordering at a yell

"Because that's what you do when you move Harper. You sell the old. What else would you do with it?" He asks in a condescending manner.

"I was going to let Jax have it. I mean he is the one who fucking paid for it. I thought it was only fair." I snap back at him.

"Why would he need it, doesn't he spend most of his time in jail anyway. I will never understand why you wasted your time with those people." He says with a disgust in his voice that I haven't noticed before, I was hurt by his opinion of them.

"Those people are my friends Tony. They took me in and were there for me when my parents weren't. They showed me what it was like to be a family." My voice was shaky and full of hurt. How the fuck could he say that shit, he knew what they were to me.

"I can give you a better family Harper, you know that. All they did was introduce you to drugs, crime and whatever disgusting fucked up shit Jax was into." His tone is sharp and there is almost a hint of jealousy wearing on his face.

"What the fuck is with you Tony?" I ask with tears running down my face.

"God dammit Harper, I know you have been fucking him again!" He said and I could hear the hurt in his voice.

"How did you find out?" I asked, without even wasting time trying to deny it.

"I saw the damn bite mark on the back of your shoulder, I'm sure you thought you hid it well, but I know I sure as hell didn't put it there. So, when I left this time, I decided I better figure something out" He confessed

"So, you thought your best solution was to pretend you didn't know, move me away and try to erase every trace of him?" I ask with anger at his actions and embarrassment at mine.

"I don't know Harper; I didn't want to lose you. I was hoping you got that fucking disgusting shit out of your system, but you aren't really acting like you have, so I guess I need to know right fucking now is, are you over him." He asks with a hint of desperation on his face. I stand there silent reflecting on the question and offended that he thinks any part of me is disgusting.

"I'm sorry Tony. I'm in love with him. I always have been" I confess through tears. The honesty feels good, but I do feel bad for hurting Tony.

"Well, I guess that's it then. I uh, I'll see myself out. Good luck Harper, you'll fucking need it." He says as he walks out

I feel a little bit of relief as he leaves, I knew moving wasn't the right choice and I was eventually going to back out. I know it was fucked up to lead Tony on like that, but I am in love with Jax, and I need to admit it. I am regretful that Tony found out in the way he did, I should have told him. Now I just need to figure out how to fix things with Jax, I said some pretty hurtful shit to him, I hope he will forgive me.

Chapter 13 Jax

I wake up to the feeling of being smacked in the back of my head.

"What the fuck!" I yell out looking up from my pillow to see who the hell hit me

"Oh, calm down son." My dad says. The bed groans as he sits down on the edge of it.

"What the hell dad?" I say a bit softer this time "What is it?"

"Well, your sister talked to me last night." He started to explain

"Dad, I don't wan…" He cut me off mid-sentence

"No, son you need to hear me. Now, you made your choices, and you got to live with them. So, it's time to man up a bit, get up and go get an honest Job. You owe that to her." He tells me and this is not really the conversation I wanted to have right now.

"It really doesn't matter anymore dad; Harper is moving to Seattle." I tell him trying to hide every bit of pain that brings me

"I know, but does she love him?" He questions knowing all too well the answer is no

"Ok dad, I'll talk to Kenny." I reassure him

SEATTLE, WHAT THE FUCK is she going to do in Seattle, I try shaking off the thoughts, but I just can't. I can't believe that Harper would fucking do that, especially after she just chewed my ass for risking us being apart, prison would be temporary. I try to stay focused on my work, Kenny gave me the full-time position, and I really want to keep it. It's not great money but its honest money. It's not too bad, it's only been a couple weeks but so far so good. I just need to be able to concentrate on work and not let thoughts of Harper get in the way.

After I got the shop cleaned up for the night I headed up front to clock out when I heard Ricky's voice echoing through the shop and I froze at his words.

"Well holy fuck, Harper Kennedy, what brings you to this side of town again?" He laughs

"I-I was hoping to find Jax." she says nervously, and I make my way to the lobby

"What are you doing here Harper?" My words came out harsher than I meant them to but seriously, what the fuck did she want.

"I-I-I was...um...I was hoping to talk to you, please." she says stumbling over her words

"I'll give you two some privacy." Ricky says as he walks into the office.

"Look, Harper, if you're here to tell me you're moving I already know so please fucking spare me." I tell her coldly as I punch my number into the system to clock off

"Um, ya about that, I...um...I'm not going" she says softly

"Probably better, you wouldn't survive the city. So, you drove all the way over here to tell me that you're not moving to a place you never even told me you were moving to?" I question her. She has sparked my curiosity, but I am still annoyed by the whole situation

"Um, well not exactly, I-I wanted to say I'm sorry, I never should have said those things to you." She confesses and I can hear the remorse in her voice.

"I'm sorry too." I say offering my apology, I can tell she has more she wants to say but an awkward silence has filled the room

"What happened Harper?" I ask

"Um...Tony knows." she says with tears forming in her eyes

"Oh. When did he... I mean how did he..." I stumble over my question, I can't see Harper telling him, but I can't figure out how else for him to know

"He's known for a while now I guess, I didn't cover well enough, and he saw marks, he knew it wasn't from him because he thinks it's disgusting" she tells me as she wipes a tear away from her cheek

"I'm sorry Harper." I say softly. I am sorry and I feel bad for Harper, but I'm also amused by the thought of that fucker's face when he made the connection. I can't believe he didn't say anything though.

"It's on me Jax I made the choice. Anyway, I just wanted you to know that I broke up with him." she says as she works to calm her emotions. It takes me a minute to processes what she just said

"Wait, you broke up with him?" I ask confused, he catches her cheating, and she is the one to call it off.

"I'm in love with you Jax, I always have been. I had a fantasy about what the picture-perfect life would be or should be and it was wrong. You are my life, and I need you; the label doesn't make it real. I am so sorry." She barely gets the words out before I take her in my arms and crash my lips against hers. I am in love with her, and I have waited so long to get her back.

"I love you too Harper, I want to spend the rest of my life with you!" I confess to her, I'll fucking get married even, I just need her.

"Come home with me" she says almost commanding me to do so. It turns me on so fucking much there is no way I would even pretend to deny her.

Chapter 14 Harper

The table feels cold against my bare skin and the shackles are tight. My bare pussy aches for his touch as I lay here waiting, the silk blindfold is soft but takes away my ability to see where he's standing only adding to my arousal. I feel his fingertips start to caress my arms; it sends sparks through my body and makes my core heat. He runs his fingertips down my back, a small gasp escapes my lips and my heart beats wildly in my chest. The throbbing between my thighs grows more intense with each touch. I feel his lips gently kiss my thigh and I moan out with intensity as he kisses and nibbles closer and closer to my hot aching core.

I feel his hot breath at my folds "MORE" I beg; my words are replaced by moans as he sucks my clit into his mouth. He is relentless and it feels so fucking good. My legs quiver and my toes start to go numb; the shackles are the only things keeping me from falling. My moans turn to screams and pants as I find myself on the edge of release. His tongue swirls hard and fast circles on my swollen clit.

"Yes" I moan out "don't stop"

My pussy starts to clench around nothing as my arousal starts to drip, my body grows weak as my orgasm rips through it. I melt into the table as I try to catch my breath. I feel Jax lean over me, he places soft kisses on the crook of my neck

"Need a break baby cakes?" He whispers in that irresistible sexy voice.

I am out of breath and my clit is still sensitive, but I am so fucking ready for him to fuck me. I feel his hard dick pressing against my thigh and his hand wrapping up in my long hair, a breathy "no" is all I can manage to get out.

"Good" he groans, his voice full of desire.

He pulls my hair back and digs his other hand into my hip. With one hard thrust he slams into me, god he feels so fucking good. He keeps his pace steady and his thrusts hard just the way I like to start. Uncontrollable moans fall from my lips as his thrusts start to get harder and faster, his grip on my hair tightens as I feel the other hand release my hip only to land with a loud *smack* on my ass cheek.

"More" I scream out as he does it again and again. My pussy starts to clench around his dick as I feel myself getting close to the edge again.

"Be a good whore and cum for me baby cakes." He says, I feel my arousal drip and my body shake as I find my release at his words.

I fucking love it when he talks like that. I feel his body collapse onto mine as he finds his release. After a few breathless minutes I feel him undo the shackles, he takes off the blindfold and carries me to the bed. His lips mold to mine in a deep passionate kiss, I don't want it to end but he breaks it, I whimper a little at the loss but all he does is smirk. He walks to the bathroom, and I hear the bath water start to run, soon the aroma of sweet Lilly's and Jasmine fill the air.

When Jax returns he extends his hand out to me, and I accept it. He escorts me to the bath and helps me in; he plants a soft kiss on my forehead before leaving me in my candle lit bathroom. The bath feels so good I debate even getting out, but I have been listening to Jax rummaging around in the kitchen and bedroom and my curiosity is killing me. When I come out of the bathroom I see Jax sitting on the bed, he had laid out a set of comfy pajamas for me, prepared a bowl of popcorn and had 2 beers on the nightstand.

"What's all this?" I ask with a smile

"It's Friday." He chuckles as he turns on the TV

My heart swells with Joy, he remembered. I put on my pajamas and crawled into bed next to him. He cupped my chin in his hand and gave me a soft kiss.

"I love you Harper. I always will." He says as he wraps his arm around me.

"I love you too Jax" I tell him as he hands me the bowl of popcorn. He picks a true crime documentary and hands me my beer. Title or no fucking title, I am happy, and I am never leaving this man again.

Liquor and Lust

Chapter 1

I woke up with my head still groggy from the night before, guilt overtook me as I became aware of my surroundings. "Shit!" I muttered under my breath as I struggle to get out as quickly and quietly as I can. "Why do I always do this!" I can't help but blurt out as I hit my hand against the steering wheel. With a heavy sigh I light up a cigarette, start my car and hope my head is clear enough to make it home. "Fuck I need coffee!" I say, as if anyone but myself is listening. As I try to navigate my way to a gas station, hungover in a town I don't know very well, I think about my hurried exit this morning. I know I should have gone back to sleep, given myself some more time to sober up, but I can never face the awkwardness of the morning after. I like to spare us both the "one night stand" talk, and besides, my walk of shame is much more appealing in the early hours of the morning with less people to witness it.

The bright lights of the gas station pull me from my thoughts. "Thank god!" I say to myself as I get out of my car getting all too excited for a lousy but cheap cup of coffee. I throw on a hoodie I had stashed in my car to cover my low-cut top from the night before and throw my long, now tangled brunette hair into a messy bun in hopes of looking a little less obvious. I grab the largest cup of coffee I can get, a handful of the travel size creamers, aspirin and a Gatorade for later.

The drive home seemed to take forever. I made it in silence because my head hurt too bad for music, but that left me vulnerable to that internal battle that lately keeps creeping into my head between myself and my moral compass. Needless to say, I was glad to pull into my apartment, it was only 5:30 AM and I was ready for a nap.

"GOOD MORNING SUNSHINE!" Lexi said as she bounced into my room at 10 AM with a delicious White chocolate latte in tow. She is the best roommate ever, and my best friend.

"I heard you sneak in before 6 this morning" she laughed "I figured you could use this"

"Thank you!" I said, with a still slightly groggy smile "I needed this!"

I took my first drink of my latte looking at her, standing there smiling with curiosity. I knew she was dying to get to hear all about my night, she always did when she wasn't able to be there. "OK,OK!" I groaned with a bit of dread in my voice at the thought of getting out of bed. I grabbed my slippers, and with coffee and cigarettes in hand we headed to the patio. This was always our gossip spot. Lexi's parents had given us some old furniture when we moved in here and that's where we spent a lot of mornings giving juicy details and trying to fight off hangovers.

"Now spill!" She demands with a smile as we get settled in.

I proceeded to tell her all the juicy, dirty gossip. It all started with Julie dragging me to a bonfire in the middle of nowhere, and that led to an incredibly steamy tailgate make-out session with a hunky cowboy which ended being tangled up in his bed sheets.

"So, it sounds like he was pretty amazing" she blurted, after she listened to my probably too detailed account of the night before.

"So fucking hot too!" I said with a smile

"Got out without waking him up?" she questioned

"As always" I said with a wink as we giggled and finished our coffee

"Good!" she exclaimed as she got up "I'll make breakfast."

I love our talks, we listen with no judgment and only give advice if its asked. We both know all too well that we spend plenty of time judging and fighting with ourselves over the choices we make that what we need from each other is someone to laugh about them with. With Lexi inside and me alone in silence again there was plenty of room for that creeping internal battle again. The questioning why I do it when I know its wrong. The wondering why I even drink anymore when it always ends the same way. I wondered how I even let myself end up in situations like I did last night, drunk at a stranger's house, in a town I don't know, without any of my friends. At least this time I had my car, that one was a crazy fucking night. I never even seemed to give much thought to any possible consequences that may occur while living this way, I just seemed to be driven by liquor and lust at this point.

"Mandy, breakfast." My thoughts are interrupted again as Lexi calls out for me. I was relieved too; it was getting too intense in my head.

"It's just frozen waffles and some scrambled eggs; I think we need to go shopping." She says with immediate laughter because we both know we survive on as few groceries as possible. With both of us working at restaurants and pizza joints we get whatever freebies we can get so we have more money for fun. Eggs and frozen waffles are about all you will find in our apartment, maybe some top ramen and cereal every now and then. Food is the least of our concerns really, we get more concerned with how were going to afford our coffee, booze and cigarette habit. However, being a girl has its perks in the getting booze department, a fact that Lexi and I diffidently use to our advantage.

"Well, I'm off to work" Lexi cheers as she puts her dishes in the sink.

"Thanks for breakfast, and the coffee!" I tell her as I give her a big hug to show my gratitude.

"No problem" she replies with her smile that always manages to light up a room.

"And stay out of your head! You're hot, he was hot, fun was had!" she hollers as she runs out the door.

Stay out of my head, right, I guess I made it a little too obvious I was feeling a bit conflicted this time. I take care of the few dishes we used and figured I should get myself cleaned up. I still smelled of stale booze and poor decisions, so I grab a clean towel out of the linen closet and head to the bathroom. "Holly shit!" is all I can manage to get out as I stood in front of my mirror, now naked, and a smirk taking over my lips as I stare at the marks left on my breasts and other various parts of my body. Hazy memories flashed through my head; they were sinful but made me grin just the same. I guess I'll be living in hoodies for a while.

Chapter 2

"Hey Mandy, hot guys over in the corner booth" Julie eagerly tells me as I exit the supply area with a tray of ranch cups and Parmesan cheese shakers I just filled.

"Ya, get it girl" Josh laughs as he makes his best attempt at a boob jiggle.

His spunk always gets the whole crew laughing and reminds me why I love working here so much. It's not just the tips I can manage to bring in, or the free pizza I can snag up at the end of the night, but the people. Josh's grandpa bought the place when Josh's dad Pete was just a baby so it's kind of a staple in this town. Pizza Pete's is known for its great pizza and home like feel, but I don't think the flirty waitresses hurt either. Pete and Josh run a tight ship, and they can be hard asses at times but they like to have fun and they pride their shop on excellent service.

I would say weekends here are the best though. Julie and I show up at 4 which gives us time to prepare for the rush and allows for Pete to be able to go home. Sam shows up at 5 to help Josh in the kitchen and together we make the perfect crew. We have all been working here since we were teenagers, so we are fast, efficient, and energetic. Perfect for the weekend rush. I take a quick glance over at my corner table to prepare myself. They look like working men, clean but a bit rough, construction maybe. I give myself the 'it's game time' pep talk and grab the water and silverware I just prepared and head over.

"Well hello gentlemen, what can I get for you tonight?" I say as cheery and flirtatious as I can flashing a smile.

"Well hello to you too" the three almost say in unison while smiling back. Julie was so right, they are incredibly sexy and a bit flirtatious, if I play my cards right, I could have a good tip coming.

"We'll take a combination and a meat lover please" Mr. Tall, dark, and smoking hot replies. His voice is low and sexy, and I can feel a blush starting to creep up in my cheeks.

"Sure thing! Would you like any bread sticks too, they are really good" I say dragging the words really good out a bit and giving them a wink in hopes they'll bite.

"If you say so then I guess we better try some" says Mr. I make rough and burly every woman's fantasy. He had broad shoulders and dusty blond hair, his beard was well kept, and his green eyes were seductive and sexy. My god how do you get three ridiculously fucking perfect men in the same friends group. This is getting me all kinds of flustered I can feel my body temperature rise with my attraction.

"Alright" I say with a giggle, "now what would you like to drink?"

I go back to the kitchen area to put in their order; I need to take a minute to catch my breath and cool down before taking them their drinks. I make it known that Julie downplayed the three of them a little which makes everyone chuckle, and me a little grateful that the hickies from a couple weeks ago have finally faded so I can show a bit of cleavage and not look unavailable. It may be slutty but I'll use anything I can to my advantage and showing off some cleavage and being flirty really brings in the tips. Bigger tips mean more coffee, cigarettes, and booze if necessary.

I continue my night making rounds through all my tables, checking in, flirting a bit here and there and watching for any drinks that need refilled. Fridays are always busy, and it can be hard to keep up sometimes but the 4 of us manage pretty well. I was so busy I didn't even realize that closing time was approaching and my table of arousal was still there.

"Well gentlemen, was everything to your liking tonight?" I ask

"It was, and the bread sticks were good." Rough and burly says with a smile and offering up a wink

"Do you need anything else?" I ask before I get their final check ready

"Maybe a phone number" the third one pipes up with a mischievous grin that makes me blush as a tingling sensation shoots straight to my core. He was athletic and lean; he had a seductiveness about him that had my heart racing.

"Oh" is all I can manage to get out followed by a slightly nervous giggle. I am pretty confident that I didn't hide that well at all.

"We're good sweetheart" tall, dark and smoking hot says in that low husky voice that literally almost takes my breath away. Holly fuck I am having a hard time hiding my attraction and desire, these guys have got to go, they are filling my thoughts with all kinds of dirty fantasies.

"Alright then" I say with a smile, "If you take your ticket to my beautiful friend Julie at the register, she'll get you all squared away" I say as I wink and walk back to the kitchen. I watch the register as I put away cups and stock silverware. I watch as Julie fails to hide her overwhelming attraction. I can't help but laugh at her stumbling over her words and unable to hide the blush taking over her pale cheeks. A small part of me wants to step in and help her because I know what she is going through, but it's too much entertainment.

As I clear the table and pick up the overly generous tip, I smile as I notice a piece of paper with a phone number and a note that reads:

sweetheart you girls should come party with us we'll show you a good time.

Fuck, that offer is tempting.

Chapter 3

"MANDY, JUST FUCKING call the guy already. You've had his number for a week now and we have to practically mop your drool off the floor every time Julie brings them up." Lexi playfully yells from the house as she makes her another cup of coffee and grabs the box of cold pizza from the fridge.

"I just don't know." I protest, I have never really been in this situation before. I mean guys ask for my number all the time, but I don't give it out. I'm not an exchange phone numbers kind of girl, it's easier that way, no commitment. I wasn't expecting them to leave one, let alone a note asking to party with them.

"They were dripping with sex appeal Mandy what's not to know?" Julie questions lifting a brow

"I just try to not intentionally hook up with customers" I say trying to change the subject knowing that it was a lame excuse, but I am only a few more seconds from giving into not only my friends but my lust driven brain as well.

"Wow" laughed Lexi, "That was lame"

I smile because I knew when I said it my friends would see right through it. I really didn't know what my hang up was about it all really. It would just be the same as any other time. Just another story, another one of Mandy's adventures as Lexi calls them. On the surface that is exactly what I wanted, a night of drunken, mindless, no strings sex. No expectations to follow, no chance of letting either of us down, a one and done deal. But why? Why was I letting that desire for lust drive me still after 3 years, and at the same time why was I all of a sudden feeling so wrong for it?

"I don't even know which one it is" I try to protest again, but at this point I already know I'm losing

"Does it really matter" Lexi asked, I knew her question came from genuine curiosity. I had made no secret of the fact that I would take any one of them or all of them for that matter. They were all gorgeous.

"Oh hell, fuck it!" I say letting my desires win out. "Where did I put that number?"

"That's my girl!" Lexi cheers as she starts to dance around the patio

"Party time!" Julie squeals almost jumping out of her chair.

I take a look around my room trying to remember where I stashed the number. I try to decide if I actually have a preference to which mystery man it might be. Is it better if I do? It probably doesn't really matter one way or the other really, it always turns into a hit it and quit it one nighter anyway. I never stick around to even see what other options someone is willing to offer. I like my freedom, it suits me, besides a girl with my history doesn't exactly scream girlfriend material. Nobody really wants to lock it down with a girl like me. I make myself another cup of coffee and make my way back to the patio.

"Here goes nothing" the butterflies fill my stomach, and my heart starts to race. I didn't think I would be this nervous.

"Hello" I hear a deep husky voice on the other end of the line that almost takes the breath right out of me and sends tingles through my body. It was tall, dark and smoking hot. A wave of excitement rushes over me and I feel giddy, I guess I did have a preference.

"Hi" I say as I catch my breath knowing that nervousness still lingers in my voice, "I-I-It's Mandy from Pete's" I say stumbling over my words like a fool, I'm really second guessing my decision here.

"Hey sweetheart, I was hoping you would call" his words put me at ease a bit and I smile so big my face hurts.

"Oh, you were huh?" I tease as my confidence starts to sneak back in.

"I was starting to think you going to decline my offer" He jokes.

"So, the offer still stands?" I ask with my voice sounding a little more excited than I wanted.

"Yes" he answers letting out a bit of a chuckle "When were you thinking?"

"How's tonight, say around 11:30?" I ask as I cross my fingers and scrunch up my face, and Lexi and Julie stare with anticipation

"Sounds great, should I call the guys or is this just a you and me kind of party?" the question sends a wave of heat through my body. The thought of me naked with him gives me a rush of arousal. I need to compose myself.

"I'm bringing friends" I giggle

"Alright then. I'll text you the address sweetheart, see you tonight."

I squeal with excitement as the phone hangs up, Lexi and Julie can't help but join in. Our squeals of excitement turn to laughter as we realize that we are getting starred at by some neighbors.

"So, the parties on, he's calling the guys" I say lighting another cigarette trying to calm my nerves "Now we got to figure out what we are taking to drink and what the fuck we're going to ware!"

Chapter 4

I could hardly wait to get off of work tonight, my stomach full of butterflies, my head full of images of that sharp jaw line and his captivating dark eyes that draw you into their gaze and keep you there. I imagine what it will feel like when I'm in his arms, with his wide chest and huge biceps wrapped around me. He was muscular, tall, tan, tattooed and imagining his naked body against mine was sending shivers through out my body and made my core ache.

"You ready Julie?" I ask with a small sense of urgency

"Clocking out now girl, keep your pants on" She teases. The statement makes a laugh escape my lips because all I can do right now is think about taking them off tonight.

My apartment is close, so we are able to hurry back and have time to freshen up before we have to head out to meet the guys. I had picked out my favorite dark blue jeans that hugged my hips and ass just right, at least that's what I'm told. I paired them with a black, low cut tank top to show off my boobs, and a pink and gray fitted flannel top. I let my long brunette hair down out of my messy bun so I can reset my curls and touched up my make up. I chose my sparkly pink flip flops, they matched my flannel top, and they were easy to grab and go on the run.

Julie had picked out a cute pair of light blue low-rise jeans to show off her lean abdomen with a pink low-cut top and a black zip up hoodie. She opted for boots instead of flip flops. Her blond hair was long and straight, and her hazel eyes really popped with the eye shadow she was wearing. She was always so pretty, and it never took much effort. She had a rocking body and long legs; she also never had any problem showing it all off. God she was so beautiful, and guys were drawn to her. She was more of a good girl though; she didn't really get around much. Don't get me wrong she liked the chase, but she also liked the commitment and benefits of relationships.

"You girls look hot!" Lexi chimes as she comes in the door

"Thanks, so do you Lex" Julie tells her

"You too babes, what did you get us to drink" I ask with excitement. We always have Lexi pick up the liquor, she always makes sure we have enough.

"I got all the goods" she laughs "I got the rum, I got the tequila, I got the whiskey, and I got the vodka. Do you think that covers it"

"Fuck ya! Julie and I got the smokes, so I guess were all set. Let's go" I say clapping my hands.

We put the address into Lexi's GPS, it's a little way out of town but only about 20 minutes. We light our cigarettes for the drive and Julie, and I crack open a bottle to start a bit of pre-game action. My nerves calm a bit as the rum and nicotine take effect. We crank the radio up when our favorite song come on and I don't think the mood could get any better. We pull up to a small house in the country, well the middle of nowhere really. Butterflies whirl in my stomach once again and my heart almost pounds out of my chest. I push Julie to knock on the door, fuck why am I so nervous, it's a one and done deal, out before morning. The door opens and my heart skips a beat, my body temperature rises, and my core starts to ache as that low, husky voice rings in my ear. "Hello Sweetheart"

I love it when he calls me that, a feeling that I have gone out of my way to avoid feeling for years now is starting to creep in. I should run now, if I don't, I will be playing with fire. I stand there at his door practically frozen and unable to move. I can hardly breathe, its real now, I'm staring him in the face. I am outside my comfort zone, and it is keeping me on edge. I want him so bad, my cheeks blush and I know he can see the desire in my eyes. This is so outside of my normal, its different than meeting some guy at a bar or a party and going home with him. This was pre planned, thought out. A hint of emotion went into this. I am starting to think I made a mistake by coming here.

"H-Hey" I stammer feeling like a fool, but my nervousness is getting the better of me. "These are my friends, Julie, who you've met and Lexi, my roommate."

"Hi ladies, I'm Issac. I guess we haven't been officially introduced. Please, come in and meet my friends."

We finally got names to put with faces, Mr. Smoking hot was Issac, rough and burly was introduced to us as Max, and seductive and athletic mystery man number 3 was James. Lexi and James seemed to be pretty smitten with each other right away, but they did seem like a great fit. They were both built like athletes, and both were incredibly good looking. Julie and Max seemed to have instant chemistry, but that wasn't too surprising because he was laying it on pretty thick at the register the night they came in. I hope this means it will be a good night.

"We brought alcohol" I say making a pathetic attempt at small talk

"That was nice" Issac says with a chuckle rumbling up in his chest "Do you want a shot glass, or do you want me to mix you a drink?"

"How about a drink" I smile

"Coming right up" he says in my ear as he grabs the bottles from my hands and I am confident he knows exactly how much he is turning me on. I don't know how long I'm going to be able to hold my shit together and not pounce.

Chapter 5

I'm only 4 drinks in and starting to feel tipsy, so far all I have done is flirted shamelessly and probably made an ass of myself. I did however manage to find out that Issac and Max own a construction company together and James owns his own landscaping business. Even through my buzz I find myself thinking about how these three incredibly gorgeous, successful men have made it this far in life with no attachments. Maybe there is something wrong with them? Maybe we should run? I can't decide if it's time for another drink or if I should sober up to shake off the silly thoughts. I take a gamble and decide on another drink.

"So handsome, can you mix me another?" I ask

"I don't think we need that at the moment" he says in a seductive manner closing the gap between us, a slightly crooked smile forming on his lips. My breath hitches in my throat as I realize in that moment that I am up against a wall, literally. He places his hand firmly on my hip as he leans in closer, I can feel my body temperature rising with his touch and his gaze locks on mine. His lips crash against mine and it sends an ache straight to my core. I wrap my hands around his waist pulling his hard body closer to mine, a small whimper escapes my lips when I feel his hardened cock pressing against me. He breaks the kiss, but only for a moment, just long enough to flash a cocky smile. I am practically mush in his arms right now.

His hands move down to grab my ass tightly pulling me closer and giving me an even better feel of what I want right now. He pins me tighter against the wall and I feel his hand travel up my body and start to wrap up in my hair, he pulls my head back to expose my neck to him, and he shows no mercy as he sucks and nibbles, I can't help but moan out with pleasure as his mouth travels toward my breasts. I can tell I am dripping with excitement now and need to feel him, all of him. I move my hands to his belt trying to gain access to his bulging cock that has been rubbing against me making me desperate to feel it inside of me.

"You sure sweetheart?" he asks, as if I would say no at this point but I find the gesture flattering. He grips my ass firmly and hoists me up, I wrap my legs around his hips as he carries me to his room. I can't help but take his earlobe in my mouth and gently bite and suck, I hear the pleasure he gets as he moans softly. I am suddenly thrown onto his bed, and I let out a small squeal in excitement. He takes off his shirt to reveal his hard tattooed body and I can feel the lust fill my eyes. The bed dips as he gets in and his large hands spread my legs as he crawls in between them. I can feel his hands grasp the button of my jeans and before I know it, they are on the floor revealing my pink lace panties. A lust filled groan escapes his lips and his eyes darken with desire. It doesn't take long before my top is bare to him, and my nipples are hardened into peaks. He takes one into his mouth and sucks hard almost to the point of pain but then releases, I am so ready for him.

He takes in the other nipple but this time nibbles, I moan out as he travels down my body kissing and nipping until he settles between my legs. He runs the pad of his thumb across my hardened clit and pleasure filled "YES" escapes me. He removes my panties and takes a languid lick before sucking my clit into his mouth.

"Oh Fuck" I barely breathe out "More"

He thrusts two fingers into my heat curving them slightly to hit my spot. He continues thrusting his fingers into me over and over as he sucks and nibbles my clit, my pussy clenches, my toes curl, my fingers dig into the sheets and uncontrollable moans fall from me as the waves of my orgasm rock through me violently. I was trying so hard to catch my breath afterwards that I missed him take his pants off. The next thing I feel is the head of his dick at my hot aching folds.

"You are so fucking wet for me" he says with so much arousal in his voice

He once again shows no mercy, he thrusts his hips forward slamming all the way into me over and over. He pinches my clit between two fingers, and I scream out, I dig my nails into his hips and a pleasure filled "Fuck" escapes his lips. He leans down to suck on my breasts, and I bury my heels into his ass to keep him deep, I move my hands to his back and bury my nails deep into his skin. My moans get louder and louder, the pleasure keeps building, and I feel close to my climax, my grip I have on him gets tighter and I beg for more. I feel his hand wrap up in my hair again as he pulls, so hard this time my head snaps back, my neck fully exposed to him, and instead of sucking and kissing he bites down hard and digs his teeth in, I don't know why but I am sent over the edge and I scream his name as my orgasm rips through me. He soon finds his release after, and we lay there practically breathless.

He pulls my naked body into his chest and places soft kisses on my temple before drifting off to sleep. A feeling of contentment rushes over me and it makes me want to run now instead of later, but my body doesn't move. I find myself sinking closer into his body, his bulging tattooed arms wrapped around me make me feel safe and happy. I glance at the clock and see its only 2 AM, a couple hours won't hurt right?

Chapter 6

I wake up in a haze, I am comfortable, still in his arms, this feels so nice. I find myself not wanting to leave, but I have to, I can't do this, I am not ready. I slowly inch my body away from his and find myself frowning at the loss of his touch. "Fuck, get it together Mandy" I whisper to myself. The bed groans a little as I stand and it stops me in my track for a minute. I check to see if it made him wake; I let out a small sigh of relief as I realize it didn't. I am quick but quiet about getting out of his room, I just hope my friends can be the same, if I can find them.

I walk through the kitchen and out to the living room trying to find Lexi and Julie. "Shit" I say, a little louder than I wanted to, when I realize it is almost 6 AM. I am relieved to see Lexi getting her shoes on.

"Where's Julie?" I whisper to Lexi; she just giggles softly and points to a doorway. There was Julie still saying goodbye to Max. It makes me laugh a little, but I am in a hurry, I have to get out of here, something is happening with my emotions, and I don't like it one bit.

"Julie, suck face later! Let's go now!" I whisper yell across the room

"OK, Ok" Julie whines as she leans in and kisses Max one more time. A sigh of relief comes as we exit the house and make our way to the car.

"Holly Shit Mandy" Lexi and Julie both say almost in unison as they stare at me with surprise

"What the Fuck happened to your neck?" Julie finishes

"Shit do I have another hickie?" I ask kind of giggling as I get in the car.

"Hickie?" Lexi loudly questions "It looks like you were attacked by a fucking vampire!"

I look in the visor mirror to see a large dark purple bruise forming, I run my finger over it and wince a little from the pain. Issac's bite, I can't hide this one with a hoodie, a blush creeps up on my cheeks and heat rushes back to my core as I remember what if felt like. The way he made me cum so violently when his face was buried between my legs. The way he slammed into me before I could catch my breath. It was rough and I loved every minute of it. The way he pulled my hair and sunk his teeth into my neck sent my pleasure over the top and opened up a whole new experience. It hurt but the pain only heightened the pleasure, and I can't help but smile ear to ear as see the aftermath in the mirror. My thighs clench together tight, and I start to crave his touch desperately.

"Earth to Mandy" Julie laughs as she taps a pack of cigarettes on my shoulder from the back seat "You look like you need one of these"

"Oh shit, sorry" I say as I am pulled from my thoughts "Thank you, I diffidently do!"

"So, about your Vampire diaries fantasy?" Lexi Jokes "I am very curious" she laughs

"Ya, me too. I wasn't aware you were a vampire fan" Julie giggles "That looks like it hurt, like a fucking lot" she laughs

"It actually made it so much better. It's weird, almost like the pain caused more pleasure." I explained "It was pretty fucking awesome actually. I do not have a vampire thing?"

"Bitch please" Julie roars out with laughter "You look like you went ten rounds with fucking Dracula, or the cast of True Blood. You so have a Vampire thing!"

"Just a new kind of thing, not a paranormal fantasy thing" I can't help but laugh but I am also kind of embarrassed. I never minded a little hair pulling even a smack on the ass every now and then, but biting was a whole new experience, and I wanted it again.

"How was James?" I ask trying to shift everyone's attention a little bit.

Lexi smiles "Well he was no bloodsucker!" She laughs "But I do have a few handprints on my ass cheeks"

"Nice" I smile

"I want to hear about Max" Lexi says to Julie

"Yes, do tell" I say

"Well, there was no ass smacking, or blood sucking" she says with laughter "But he was good. He did amazing things with his hands, and he refused to finish himself until I was completely satisfied. So, he was kind of romantic." She said with a completely satisfied look on her face. "He also asked me on a date!" she said with a squeal.

"That's great Julie" Lexi says

"It was a fucking good night then for all!" I say.

"Ya, but now the big question Mandy. Are you going to see him again?"

"I-I-I don't know?" I say but it comes out sad and my heart clenches a little in my chest at the thought of not seeing him again. This feeling right here is why I don't do things that way, why no emotion can go into it. I should have known better. I know it never ends well when you go catching feelings.

"Well clearly you think he is great in bed Mandy, so he could be like your blood sucking fuck buddy or something" Julie says with laughter

I giggle in response because it really was funny, but I am so confused. I have realized I actually like him, so now what, I am kind of broken, and I always end up getting hurt. I have major trust issues, and I diffidently have a less then desirable reputation. I'm not exactly the kind of girl men choose to date. I'm fun, drunk, and slutty. So basically, I'm a take home for a night not a take home to mama. I have thrived this way, I chose it proudly, I was fine with it. Up until a few weeks ago that is, I don't know what changed.

right now, all I want to do is tell Lexi to turn the car around go back. I need to feel him again, I want too, but I am so afraid it won't work. What if he was only thinking it was a one and done deal too?

"I just don't think that would be a good idea. It never ends well" I chime in

"By the looks of you it would be fun" Lexi says with a smile

"I would just get hurt in the end" I say without being able to stop myself. My friends just stared at me looking a bit confused. And then Lexi's face fell a little bit

"You like him" Lexi says

My face drops with a bit of sadness, and I light another cigarette and shake my head yes.

"It was fun but moving on" I say a tears threaten to prick my eyes. Fuck, this is so stupid. What is wrong with me?

As we pull into the apartments I put out my cigarette out and head inside. I need to sleep this off and get my head right. I slip off my jeans and my flannel, toss my hair up. I finish of a bottle of water I had on my nightstand, curl up in my bed and wait for sleep to take over.

Chapter 7

I wake up feeling empty and full of regret, I was really hoping this feeling would pass. I see a note from Lexi that reads:

Hey girl, grabbing food be back soon, I made coffee, drink some and take a hot shower it will help.

I figure I will take her advice, well the coffee part anyway. My bed groans as I make myself get up and get out of it. I find my slippers and my robe so I can make my way to the kitchen. I pour me a cup of coffee and debate with myself if I should add a shot to it. I decide against it and head back to my bed, I kind of want to hide here today. I pick up my phone from the bedside table and see that I have missed messages and calls. My heart sinks as I see the calls are from Issac along with a message:

Hey sweetheart, I was hoping you would be here when I woke up, Max said you left in a hurry this morning. I'm sorry if I was too rough. I want to see you again.

Waves of emotion run through me as I read his words. Did he really want me to stick around? How could he possibly think he was too rough, I screamed his name in such pleasure last night and I loved every bit of it, but then I ran, I ran like I always do. This time I am fighting with an emotional train wreck instead of my moral compass.

I caught feelings, for the first time in three years I like someone. Not only do I like him, but I slept with him when I was fully aware that I might. I broke so many rules I had set for myself. Regret instantly consumes me and my heart twists in my chest, tears fill my eyes, and I can't hold them in. I should have known this would happen one day, did I really think that I could go around being a slut the rest of my life with no consequence.

Why couldn't I have been normal back then, it was just a breakup for Christ sake. A breakup at 19 even, but I was so in love with him and it crushed my soul. We had been together for so long by then and I really thought it would be forever. Troy promised me it would be forever. He was my first and I thought it was the real deal even though we were young, but it blew up in my face. He played me, well me and Rachel, and all the girls he slept with while he was with us. I was so devastated when I found out about Rachel, but I was completely destroyed when we found out about all the other girls he had. It was like I shut down completely, I broke.

After I came out of hiding, I had changed, I never wanted to feel that way again. I decided I wasn't going to fall for a man again so I could avoid another broken heart. I thought about tiring to only date losers, they bring nothing to the table so you couldn't really get attached, but I opted against it.

One night Lexi tried to cheer me up, so she dragged me out of the house to a party way out in the sticks. Josh and a couple of his friends knew some people who lived out there and it was supposed to be a pretty big party. It was the perfect place for a bunch of 18- to 20-year-old kids to go drink, have a good time and not get busted, so we tagged along. That's the night that I discovered the one and done approach.

We were all drinking and dancing by the light of the fire, and I got really cozy with a good-looking stranger. Next thing I knew we were in the back of his truck, and I was giving into my body's desires. I couldn't resist the way his hands explored every curve of my body, the way they gently settled on my breast as he caressed my hardened nipples. I loved the way his hot breath felt against my ear as he sucked on my earlobe. I was begging for more when his hand found its way down into my panties and rubbed my aching clit. I moaned out with such pleasure as

I rode his dick to my climax that night, in a truck bed under the stars, with so many possible witnesses. After the party my friends and I got in the car and left. The next morning, I was left satisfied with sore hips, and a hangover, as well as no chance of a broken heart. From then on it was my no strings, no commitment life.

I knew I was playing with fire with Issac, but I did it anyway, now I have feelings for him and it already hurts. The thought of a relationship scares the shit out of me but the thought of being just fuck buddies makes my heart hurt just as much as the thought of not seeing him again. Would he even want me if he knew the reality of who I was? Would he even trust me to be faithful? My head is pounding, and I can't tell if it's the hangover or the uncontrollable emotional roller coaster that I'm on that is the cause of it. I need this breakdown to stop, I decide that maybe Lexi was right, and a good hot shower will help me.

Chapter 8

I sat on the porch in my robe smoking, waiting for Lexi to get home hoping she could talk some sense into me. The hot shower offered a small amount of relaxation, but I still could really use my friend right now. I feel a small sense of relief as I hear the door.

"Hey Mandy" Lexi offers up softly as she sits down next to me

"Hey" I say in response looking at her through swollen sad eyes

"So, what will it be, the ice cream and cookies, the pain killers, or the Jack Daniels?" she questions knowing that I will in no doubt need one of the three.

"I'll start with the cookies and pain killers, then maybe the ice cream and Jack" I say knowing that for the way I'm feeling right now it may take everything we have.

"Oh shit, that bad huh?" Lexi says as she places the open package of Oreo's on the table and prepares me two Tylenol "I'm going to text Julie 911, this looks like it will be an all-hands-on deck kind of night" she adds as she heads into the kitchen to grab some glasses and soda.

I swallow my two Tylenol down with my last bit of coffee and dig into the cookies. I should probably eat real food but right now I feel like playing into the stereotype of the brokenhearted.

"So, Julie is on her way" Lexi says as she sets down a few glasses and a case of soda.

"Thank you, Lex." I say offering up a half smile. I really do love that she went to all this trouble to be prepared for whatever I was going to be feeling. I really do have the best friends.

"Any time girl! So, you want to talk about it?" she asks softly handing me a cigarette she lit for me

"Maybe after we smoke." I say

"Fair enough" she said handing me a can of soda, I offer her a genuine "thank you" in return, set the can down and continue smoking. The silence was nice, so I took my time to delay the inevitable.

"Well spill" Lexi says once my cigarette is out

"I don't know. I am so confused. Issac called, and then messaged when I didn't answer" I say trying to keep my emotions calm.

"Oh. Well how did that go?" she asked as she opens the can of soda, she handed me earlier and starts to pour it in our glasses

"I haven't responded yet" I say as I shove another Oreo in my mouth

"I see" she says gently as she cracks the bottle of Jack open. I know she is filled with curiosity but not wanting to push too hard. I look over at her and make eye contact. She offers a warm smile, but I can see her question all over her face.

"I don't know what to say to him" I say answering the unasked question that was lingering in the air

"Well, what did he say?" she asked and about that time Julie comes barging through the door. Man, it didn't take her long.

"I'm here, I got the 911!" Julie says as she hands out our burgers and fries. A small giggle finally escapes me because her sense of urgency in the matter is quite funny

"Thank you, Julie," Lexi and I exclaim as we each start munching on a handful of fries

"So, Mandy, getting back to the point" Lexi says, "What did Issac say in his message?" she questions not letting the interruption actually interrupt the conversation at hand.

"He said Max had told him I left in a hurry, so he hoped he wasn't too rough, and he wants to see me again" I reply

"So that means he likes you right?" Julie questions

"I don't know. What if he only wants to fuck around for a while?" I say trying to keep my emotions in check, but it is getting so damn hard for me to fight back the sadness.

"I think you are more worried about falling in love with him and having it end than anything else Mandy" Lexi says, and it makes my heart clench in my chest. She was so right, it scared me.

"I really don't think I could handle that. I also like him way too much already to just fuck around." I say fighting back tears

"Maybe you could get a better feel of the situation if you called him or messaged back" Julie says in a soft almost timid tone

"I know you are probably right, But then what? I tell him Hey so I like you but just thought you should know I'm a broken mess with trust issues and have guarded my heart for three years by being a slut." I say with sarcasm and sadness

"Mandy, I understand that you have been around and that might not be what all guys want but let's look at the reality for a quick minute. They just did the same thing that we did. Do you really think this was Issac's first time? I'm going to say no; he's probably a man whore. They are 29-year-old single men who own their own businesses, they have probably fucked a lot of girls." Lexi says pretty matter of fact, which stings a little bit, but I know she is trying to make a point, and it was a good one. Issac had probably been whoring around more that I have been.

"It's still different for guys." I say

"You're right, but he may not care as much as you think he will, or even perhaps as much as you do." Julie chimes in

"Mandy, you can't change what you have done up until now, you can't let regret start to consume you. All you can do is try to move forward and do something different" Lexi points out.

I know both of my friends are right and I might be over thinking it, but it won't change the fact that I have issues. It also won't change the fact that if things go sour, I will be devastated and probably become worse than I am now. Can I really survive another downhill spiral?

"I know you guys are probably right. I am just really scared to get hurt again; it broke me" I cry

"I know it did, and if it were to happen all over again Lexi and I will be there right by your side again, just like last time. I think you should give it a shot with him, just call. I think your fucking neck might need a break though." She laughs handing me another drink

"Well said Julie, well said. It's a fucking big bruise" Lexi says raising her glass with laughter.

"Alright, I will think about it, no more sadness, let's eat some cookies!" I say shoving another Oreo into my mouth.

Chapter 9

"It's been a week, Mandy; don't you think you should face him. I think he really likes you." Julie says as we lock up Peat's for the night

"I don't think I'm ready yet, it's a loaded conversation." I say trying to keep things short. I know her and Lexi mean well and I know they are right; I do need to talk to him but it's so hard. I have been trying to avoid emotions like the plague for years now and last weekend was like a brick to the face from it all, I just needed a little more time.

"Mandy, I know I don't offer much advice to you ever but if I can interject here" Josh pipes up on the way to his car "You have been ghosting him for a week now. If that were me, I would be taking it as a hint that you're not interested in me and moving on. If you want to be with him, and I am pretty sure you do, tell him. If it doesn't work, you will be in the same place you are now."

"Josh, let me ask you, if it was you how would you react to my way of life? Am I really the kind of girl you would want a relationship with?" I ask

"Yes Mandy, and I'll tell you why. He had you pegged from the minute he left his number at the table. You drove the point home when you called him and wanted to meet up, and he sure as hell knew the kind of girl you were when you fucked him. You're not a bad person Mandy, you may feel broken but you are kind and funny that's what he sees in you." Josh's words rolled out bluntly. I couldn't even get a response out before he got in his car and drove away.

"Will you come with us Mandy?" Julie asked

"You guys go ahead and go. I'll think about it and maybe meet you there?" I say to Julie as I get in my car and head home. I am in need of a hot shower and some relaxation after this week. I also need to reflect on what Josh said. Did Issac really know ahead of time how I was; did I really have an "I'm a slut" ora about me, or did he just hope? Was he really looking for a girl like that or did he really see me for who I was under the front I put on? So many more questions flood my already exhausted brain.

I PUT ON MY FAVORITE fluffy pink robe and mix a strong drink after I get out of the shower. I decide to see if there is anything good on Netflix to binge watch. My show searching is interrupted when I hear a knock on my door. Who the fuck would be here this time of night, and my heart stops when I hear that deep, sexy as fuck voice say my name.

"Mandy, come on, please talk to me" Issac pleads

"Uh, ok, uh, come in" I holler from the couch

"Why are you avoiding me, Mandy?" he asks, his tone is sharp, and I feel almost sad that he didn't call me sweetheart.

"I-I-I" I stumble, and I can find words to explain

"I was worried I scared you off, worried I hurt you, Max said your neck looked pretty bad. Lexi tells me that's not the case, and Julie told me to come over here so you can tell me. So, what is it?" He asks with a softer tone

"I-I- I didn't know that you wanted me to stay." I say and I feel regret at my words. I need to be completely honest.

"OK. That explains why you left. That doesn't explain why you didn't call, or text." he says

"That's only part of the reason I left." I start to explain I can feel the tears start to creep in, here goes nothing

"I got scared, I ran, I always run, I never stay." I say and tears start to fall. He walks over to sit next to me. He rubs soothing circles on my back, his touch calms me, and my tears slowly fade.

"I knew you were a runner sweetheart; I could tell. It was pretty obvious when James asked for a phone number, so I left mine and gave you the power to choose. I thought that when you called me it meant you were interested in more. I was hoping it meant you wanted to try not running." His words bring comfort and confusion all at the same time. He likes me, wants a relationship, but he wanted that with someone like me.

"So, you want to be with me because I'm a hoe?" I ask confused

"Don't say it like that." He says sharply "I don't have a great reputation myself. I like sex, I've had a lot of it with a lot of different women. I am wanting to settle down a bit and have something real with someone, but I need someone who understands me. I like you Mandy and I want to be with you" He confesses

"I am so scared. I really like you, but I don't want to get hurt again." I tell him

"Sweetheart, I can't promise I will never hurt you, but I can promise it won't be on purpose. I just know I want you to be mine." His words are fair, that's probably all either of us can promise right now. I want to be his, only his.

"Ok" I tell him "So what now?"

"Well," he says coyly as he closes the gap between us "I want to kiss my girl now" he says leaning in.

I smile and let his lips crash against mine. Butterflies fill my stomach and my heart races. I can feel my body temperature rise with excitement. I love kissing him. He pulls me up onto his lap and desire consumes every inch of my body. I wrap my fingers in his hair and deepen the kiss. We are going to have to move this heated make out session to the bedroom.

Chapter 10

Heat rushes to my core as I start to travel down his hard tattooed body planting open mouth kisses all the way down to his waist. I nibble and tease a little bit before unbuttoning his pants to free his hardened cock from his jeans. I take a long hard suck and then another before climbing over him. His eyes darken with lust as I line my heated folds over the head of his dick before gliding slowly down. A soft moan escapes my lips as I feel him against my walls and take him in all the way to the hilt. My pussy clenches around him as I glide easily up and down over and over. He feels so fucking good. His hand travels up to my breast to roll my hard nipples between his fingers. "Yes, more" I breath out desperate to feel what I felt last time.

His large hand moves from my breast to my throat and grips firmly, I moan loudly with pleasure at the sensation of it and my pace on his dick quickens. "Harder" I moan out unable to control it, I need him to fuck me harder. He firmly grabs me and flips me underneath him. He pulls all the way out and his large hands dig into my hips; he thrusts back into me deep over and over. "Fuck" I scream out as my nails run down his chest making him moan out in pleasure at the sensation. He takes my nipple in his mouth and sucks hard before biting into my breast. The waves of my orgasm rock through me and he keeps thrusting and thrusting until he too finds his release and fills me. He gently kisses my breast and then pulls me in close to him, making sure plant soft kisses on my temple. I melt into his arms loving the feeling of being held. Contentment consumes me and I drift off to sleep.

I wake to find Issac's strong arms still wrapped around me. His hard naked body is still molded against mine. I feel like I could lay here forever, just like this, soaking this all in.

"Good morning sweetheart" he whispers in my ear

"Good morning" I say before planting a passion filled kiss on his lips. I am so happy to wake up together

"You want me to make coffee?" he asks

"I would love coffee, but I can make it." I say as I start to get up to find my clothes

"I'll make it sweetheart" he says as he kisses my forehead

"Thank you" I say as I lean in for one more kiss

I groan a little at the loss of his touch, but I really do want some coffee. I grab a tank top, and my pink flannel pajama bottoms out of my dresser and throw my long tangled brunette hair into a quick messy bun. As I leave my room to head to the kitchen I am met with the smell of more than just coffee, when I get to the kitchen I discover why.

"Oh Damn!" James exclaims "You weren't fucking kidding"

"I told you!" Lexi laughs "She had to resort to turtlenecks under her work shirt this time"

"Fucking blood sucker" Julie laughs and a blush creeps up in my cheeks

I feel Issac's arms wrap around my waist and he kisses my neck, and just like that my core heats with desire again.

"It looks fucking sexy on her doesn't it?" he says proudly

"Thanks" I blush

"Y'all look like you worked up and appetite, get some food" Max says "I worked hard on this" he laughs

"I am really hungry" I say "I didn't realize we had pancake batter" I add

"You don't" Max laughed "I brought supplies. I was warned about your lack of food"

"Hey, we have eggs" I laugh

"I felt ya'll needed a real breakfast" Max says

"Thank you, Max., I fucking love pancakes" I say as I take my heaping plate and cup of coffee over to the table. We lack chairs for everyone, so I take my new place smack dab on Issac's lap.

I look around our now crowded apartment and my heart is filled with happiness at the view. New relationships, good food, and laughter. I guess this is what it's all about. I didn't envision myself ever being in this place again, but I am happy that I am. I somehow feel complete, less broken, maybe even a little bit normal. Now if I can just avoid fucking it all up it will be a great happy ever after.